Disjointed CUSTODY

A Novel

BRIAN W. SMITH
ELAINE FLOWERS

BeforeYouPublish Book Press
—— We Publish Books ——

Published by:
Before You Publish – Book Press
Addison, TX

Cover Designs: Brian W. Smith
Edits: In House at Before You Publish – Book Press

Published and printed in the United States of America

First Edition
ISBN-13: 978-0-9747388-7-1

Smith, Brian W.
Flowers, Elaine
Disjointed Custody – First edition

www.BeforeYouPublish.com

Disjointed Custody

Prologue

MELISSA

My demons hadn't shown up for a long time. Things, I thought, were good. It was a Friday in December, and Ryan and I had been out all morning Christmas shopping for Suni and other family members. We were hosting Christmas for the first time that year. Our families would be joining us at our newly built home.

There was a chill in the Dallas air that made the mood for shopping perfect. We had hit the malls hard and had a great time doing it. We worked as a team— like best friends and it was just like old times. Even when we didn't agree on what to get someone, we came up with a system of compromise that had things going smoothly. There was nothing like the holidays to highlight the love between husband and wife. We came home, made out in the car while parked in the garage, satisfying each other in a way that came easy to us.

"I'm so behind on the design work for my clients." I pulled up my jeans, struggling to get them zipped while seated. "It's gonna be a long night so just order pizza for you and Suni for dinner, okay?"

Ryan didn't bother to zip up his khakis and stepped out of the car. "I think you forgot, sweetie. She's going to Kelly's house after school today." He grabbed bags and packages from the back seat.

"Was that tonight?" I said just before I hopped in my own car.

Ryan gave me this questioning look. It was an expression that had a way of making me feel inadequate. "You spoke to her mother last night, remember?"

"Oh. It just slipped my mind." I was sure he was right. For half a second, I tried recollecting a phone conversation, but I hit the garage button, started my car, and blew him a kiss as I backed out. I didn't have time to think about it at the moment. My mind was on work. The interface on the draft was off but I hadn't figured out how to fix it and the client wanted me to manipulate the image more. All of this should've been done yesterday but would surely take two more days for me to complete.

My mind was working to solve design problems while I took the thirty-minute drive to the office. I pulled into my parking space, and then realized I'd left my laptop on the kitchen counter. I dialed Ryan's number but disconnected before he could answer. Ryan was taking the day off so I wanted to ask him if he'd just bring it to me but the forgotten phone conversation with Kelly's mother and forgetting my computer would make him worry. I turned around and started another thirty-minute drive, headed back home.

When I turned the corner, I was hoping Ryan would be gone but I saw the car of his homeboy, Gerald, parked in front of the house on the street. At least Ryan wouldn't question my forgetfulness in front of company, so I was cool with that. He would bring it up later but for now, I was happy to have Gerald as a distraction. In fact, I was hoping to slip in and out without being noticed, if at all possible.

I pulled into the driveway, dashed out of the car and up the walkway, and unlocked the front door. It all happened so quickly and, in a blur, but what I saw never left me.

It's strange how simple things get lost in your mind and horrible things haunt you every waking moment. Eating a sandwich or watching a television program will bring it all back to you at the most inopportune times. The way someone turns a phrase and the haunting is back. A certain smell will remind you and everything is fresh as if it is happening all over again.

The image attached itself to me like a second layer of skin. Gerald leaning over the stair railing with his pants around his ankles, Ryan, my husband, standing behind him grunting. The two of them were zoned out in agonizing passion. Neither of them knew I was there until my keys hit the marble floor.

I do remember the police arriving and what came next was me being admitted into the hospital. My demons were back.

Chapter 1

RYAN

Beads of sweat bubbled on my forehead, fell to the bridge of my nose, and mingled with the manicured whiskers that aligned my quivering top lip. One droplet turned into ten and those ten morphed into dozens. Under the glow of the newly installed vanity lights in my bathroom, the perspiration became so pronounced that I appeared to have chickenpox.

My heart sputtered like the motor of an old grumpy lawnmower. I hadn't felt that flustered in a decade. Truth be told, the last time my emotions were that hard to corral was when I waited for seemingly hours to get the results of my first HIV test.

"Ryan, baby," Gerald said affectionately as he slid behind me and wrapped his arms around my waist, "you need to relax. Everything is going to be okay."

Deep down, I knew he was right, but faith and angst can't coexist. They clash like oil and water, Crips and Bloods, Fred Sanford and Aunt Esther. Although I'd prayed for forty-eight hours that faith would rise and stomp out all signs of angst, it didn't happen. Based on the damp face looking back at me in the mirror, angst was kicking faith's ass and it wasn't even close.

"I know," I muttered. "I just want this weekend to be perfect."

Gerald slid from behind me and wedged himself between my body and the bathroom countertop. He adjusted my collar and used a washcloth to dab my face.

"Boy, you are sweating like a runaway slave."

"That's because I'm as nervous as one."

"You shouldn't be because Suni adores you. There isn't a thing you can say or do that will change that. From the moment she opened her little eyes, you've let her know she's your top priority."

"Honestly, I'm not worried about how she will feel about me. I'm concerned about how she will react to you. I mean, I just want—"

Gerald muffled my speech by gently placing his index finger on my lips.

"She's an 8-year-old child. I'm expecting it to take a while for her to warm up to me. There will be times during this weekend when I'll try to touch her, and she'll pull away. When you leave the room, she'll probably be on your heels." Gerald placed his hands on my chest and kissed my lips. Even for that split second, he closed his eyes and dove into the gesture like I was headed to war and the probability of me not returning was high. "But you know what? It doesn't matter because I'm not goin' anywhere. It's time for your daughter to meet me. It's time for her to know, and to see, how her family dynamics have changed. She now has three parents who care for her. As far as how long it will take before she accepts me—we can't predict that. However, I promise you, I'm going to be the adult in this situation and give that baby all the time she needs to adjust."

And there you have it. That one exchange is a microcosm of the peace Gerald brought to my world. No matter the situation, he was the calming force. When Melissa and I split up, he was right there waiting to catch me. When I lost my job weeks before my divorce, he deposited ten thousand dollars into my savings account so that at a minimum, I could prove to the judge I had a nest egg to fall back on until I found a new job. He's my rock—the most dependable person I know.

The chime of the doorbell cut through our thin walls and rang in our ears.

"You ready?" Gerald asked.

"No."

"That was rhetorical," Gerald said and smirked. He gave me another peck and shoved me out of the bathroom. "Go get your daughter. I'll wait in the bedroom for you to come get me when you're ready."

I've seen interviews of inmates discussing the lonely feeling they have when the prison door slams and a correctional officer escorts them down the long walkway to their cell. I couldn't be sure if the anxiety I felt rivaled the inmate walk, but those sweat beads Gerald wiped away came back with a vengeance.

Take a deep breath. Be calm. She will feel your energy so give off good vibes. Melissa is an hour late. If I was this late, she'd have a conniption. Do not argue with her. Just get your baby and close the door.

"Good morning," I said with a smile so wide and fake it made my jaws ache.

"I know, I know, I'm late. We overslept and then I had a hard time getting little Ms. Thing here to put on her clothes. And then the traffic—"

"It doesn't matter," I said and waved dismissively. "What's important is that you're here and safe."

Suni looked like someone returning home from an all-night bender. She used the back of her hand to obliterate the sleep in her eyes.

"Hey, Daddy."

I pulled my drowsy child close and kissed her forehead. My nostrils welcomed Suni's familiar scent. It's a combination of powder and the Blue Magic Coconut Oil Melissa lathered her scalp with.

"Hey, baby," I whispered. "I'm glad you're here."

"Nice condo," Melissa uttered in that snarky tone she used when itching for a fight. "When I met you, you were waiting tables at Olive Garden, struggling to get through law school, and slumming with rats and roaches in that house in Oak Cliff. Now look at you—living it up in a condo in *Uptown Dallas*." The catty inflection in her voice punctuated the words 'Uptown' and 'Dallas'. "Must be nice. Ambulance chasing seems to be working out for you."

Don't take the bait. Remain polite. Grab your child and smile at this crazy bitch so she can get on her way.

"I can't complain. Is that her overnight bag?"

"Yeah. I double checked to make sure she packed everything she needs: pajamas, underwear, and a new toothbrush."

"That's fine. I already have all of those things in here for her."

"Yeah... I bet you do." Melissa craned her neck to try to see inside. "So, are you going to invite me in, or you gon' make me stand out here in this nippy weather?"

I adjusted my body to block her view. "Maybe the next time. I still have some painting and cleaning to do in the living room area."

Melissa scrunched her face and nodded. She nibbled on her bottom lip for a second and then snapped her finger.

"I almost forgot," she said and moved swiftly to her idling car. She opened the back door and came back to the door. "I have some cash here in case she needs spending money."

I wanted to tell her to keep that wrinkled ass twenty-dollar bill, but I knew it would trigger an argument that would linger for the remainder of the weekend.

"Cool," I said and took it. "The last thing I want is to have her miss a meal because of low funds."

Snarky? Yes. When you spend every waking moment dissecting your words like a politician's speech writer—making sure every word is perfect and can't be misconstrued—an occasional jab will slip out. Sue me... I'm human.

Things weren't always this tense between Melissa and me. When we first met, we were inseparable. We prayed for each other. Served as in-house professional and personal consultants. Finished each other's sentences. It was an unbreakable union—one designed to weather life's storms during that time. But things changed. What started off as a lifetime faltered after a few seasons. The proverbial *thin line* that separates love and hate had been crossed and nothing remained, but earth scorched like the suburban lawns in the Dallas area during the dog days of summer.

"Okay. I'll be back around five on Sunday evening."

"She'll be ready." I looked down at my baby. Her head was pressed against my waist. "We're going to have a great weekend. You ready to have a good time, baby girl?"

"Daddy, I'm hungry."

"If you'd gotten out of bed when I told you—"

"It's okay," I said, palm raised. "I'll make sure she gets something to eat."

"I just don't want her making it sound like I ain't feedin' her or something."

"Melissa, I know how much you care about this child and how much you do to make sure she's taken care of. There is nothing she can say that would make me believe you don't feed her."

Was my tone patronizing? Probably. Did I believe what I'd just said? Partially. Sometimes, I just didn't know when it came to Melissa. She could be a little *flighty*. I often wondered if she took her contempt for me out on Suni. Of course, I didn't say that to her; she's the biggest hothead I know. If I'd even suggested she might have displaced anger issues she'd go all *Housewives of Atlanta* on me—side-eye looks, rolling necks, snapping fingers, and tossing drinks in my face. I didn't need that shit in my life, so I just shut up.

The one thing I've learned since becoming an attorney is to treat cancer like cancer and warts like warts. The moment you start treating warts like cancer you lose perspective. With the help of Gerald—my soulmate and sounding board—I've learned to keep that perspective in mind when dealing with my crazy ex-wife.

At that moment, Gerald showed once again why I'd be lost without him. Because of the way I was positioned in the doorway, the front of my body was the only thing Melissa could see. I could feel a hand go into my back pocket.

"Her birthday gift," Gerald whispered like a stage director hiding behind a curtain whispering lines to the actor with stage fright. With a playful pinch of my butt he said, "Give it to her."

"Melissa, I want you to go enjoy your weekend. As a matter of fact, I bought you something." I dug into my pocket and pulled out the gift that was as much of a surprise to me as I was sure it would be to her. "It's a

Starbucks gift card." I had no idea how much money was on the gift card so I didn't bother to say. "I didn't get a chance to get you a gift for your birthday last week, but I didn't forget about you."

"Well, technically you did forget—which is why I'm just getting this today." Melissa opened the flap and looked at the amount written on the inside. "Twenty-five dollars. Very generous. Thanks."

She always has some kind of flip-ass remark. Can't ever just accept a gift graciously. She gets on my damn nerves...

"You're right," I blurted out after feeling Gerald's loving finger poke me in the ribs. "I got so busy with a case that I'm working on that I missed your birthday. Blame it on my head not my heart." I grabbed Suni's hand. "Now, we're going to get settled in and start our weekend."

I took a slight step backward and placed my free hand on the doorknob with the hopes Melissa would get the hint. It seemed to take a few seconds for my non-verbal communication to register with her, but eventually she seemed to catch on.

"Well, I'm gon' get going," Melissa said and leaned in to kiss Suni. "You be good this weekend."

Suni nodded.

"Okay, I'm gon' let y'all have your time."

Yeah, now back your crazy ass up before this door smacks you in the nose, I thought. Trust me, it was only a thought. I wouldn't dare say it.

Melissa backed away cautiously, the way parents do when they drop their children off at daycare for the first time. When she was on the sidewalk, I closed the door. I rested the back of my head on the door and thanked God for muzzling my words.

Suni leaned back her forehead against my stomach. The poor child was out on her feet. Had she turned around and opened those gorgeous round eyes of hers, she would have seen her lean, well-groomed, and divinely handsome *other daddy,* who'd been standing behind the door orchestrating my performance—he the ventriloquist, me the dummy.

"What you want to eat?"

"Pancakes."

"With bacon and eggs?"

"Umm hmm."

"I'm going to make that happen for you, okay?"

Suni nodded.

"Who takes care of you?"

"You," Suni replied softly.

"Who loves you?"

"You."

"Do you mind if someone came to breakfast with us?"

Suni nodded her head.

"Good," I said and glanced over at Gerald, who was fidgeting and wringing his hands like a defendant waiting for the jury to return with a verdict. I offered a comforting smile. "Suni, baby, I want you to look at me. I need to introduce you to the person who is going to eat breakfast with us."

Suni lifted her head. She looked me in the eyes and then turned around. Gerald took a step forward.

"Hello, Suni," Gerald said.

"Baby, this is Gerald... Daddy's husband."

Chapter 2

MELISSA

I was on my third shower since waking up that morning. Water, as hot as I could stand it, and suds sliding down my body felt so good. A shower before I ran three miles. A shower after I ran three miles. And another for washing off paint residue. As normal as it felt, I knew it wasn't. So, I promised myself I wouldn't take another one until the next day.

I'd had a great weekend and it had been a long time since feeling that good. Met my deadlines on Friday, and with those few days to myself, I accepted a date with a great guy—and even got me some. I rearranged all the closets, painted Suni's room, and now I was waiting on her daddy to drop her off.

As much as I loved having time to myself, I missed my baby when she was gone. But some free time was just what I needed. Will, my new man, had asked me out many times, but honestly, I just wasn't ready. I was still too angry to move on. If Ryan could fool me, then how could I ever trust a man again? I truly didn't see one sign that Ryan would ever be attracted to men. I just didn't see it. I thought things were good—not just good, but healthy between us. Hell, his face was between my legs mere moments before he was riding that dude's ass.

Whew... One... Two... Three...

Anyway, I had a great weekend. It had been a long time since I had the attention of a man and getting it made me move past some things. I had to admit I felt some type of way when I saw Ryan's condo. The mere fact he'd screwed me over so royally should've meant that hard times were coming his way. I fully expected God to rain down some serious Sodom and Gomorrah punishments on him. I wanted to see him regretful and struggling. But there he was, looking good, looking happy, and living well. So, me getting some good dick lessened the sting.

I still can't decide if the sex was good because it was, or because I hadn't had any in so long. I guess next time Will and I hook up, I'll know for sure.

I stepped out the shower, ran a fluffy white bath towel over every limb and crevice, and covered myself in Stress Relief body lotion from Bath & Body Works. I rubbed and inhaled. Rubbed and inhaled. I heard my phone buzzing on the nightstand in my bedroom and raced to it. I didn't want Ryan to think I wasn't home and try to keep Suni. He requested more visitation time than the judge awarded him and the last thing I needed was for him to decide to take me back to court, accusing me of non-compliance.

I rolled over on top of my comforter, landing on the other side of the bed, only to find a picture of Mama staring back at me on the screen.

"Hey, Diva," I answered.

"Hey, baby. How you feeling today?" She was always worried.

"Good."

"What are you up to?"

"Just running around here—Suni should be home in a minute—getting out of the shower—I painted her room—you know she loves pink, so I painted three walls pink and one a bold red and then I painted her dresser with the same red—she's going to love it."

"Wow... You sound like you're in a good mood. You okay?"

"What do you mean?"

"You been taking your medicine, Melissa?"

"Well—um—yeah."

"Are you sure? I know you forget sometimes."

"I'm great. You wanna stop by and see Suni's room? She should be here in a minute—I'm putting you on speaker so I can throw my clothes on—you want to stop by?"

"Maybe I will. I can't picture pink and red walls."

I stood inside my closet, searching through clothes, yelling, "She's gonna love it. Maybe I'll make a pot of chili—you want some chili? Where's Daddy?"

"He's still at his Mason's meeting—"

"Maybe I'll grill some steaks—I think I have steaks in the freezer—only if he's coming. Do you think he wants a steak—he can come later..."

"Baby, you sure you're okay?"

"I'm good, Mama," I said a little slower, and then exhaled. "Give me about an hour or so—I'll get my chili going—or steaks—I don't know—Suni should be here and I'll get her unpacked and settled in—okay?"

"Okay, baby. I'll be there."

Before I could say goodbye, the doorbell rang.

"I think that's them. I'll see you shortly." I was still yelling in the direction of my phone.

I pulled my wet hair up into a ponytail, slid a clean sweatshirt over my head, and raced down the stairs. I could see my baby standing in one of the double-hung windows on either side of the front door. I felt awesome, and I was eager for Ryan to see just how awesome I felt. Not that he'd care but that wasn't the point. I needed him to see that he's not the only one doing just fine.

I snatched open the door, snatched up my baby in a bear hug, and held my hand up, stopping Ryan from stepping foot inside.

"Hi, baby."

"Hi, Mommy."

"Did you have a good time?" I asked but I really didn't want to hear her go on and on about how much fun she had with him.

I took Suni's bag from Ryan's hand and noticed the smirk on his face. I imagined him saying to himself, *This chick is so tit-for-tat, not letting me in my own house because I didn't let her in my new spot. Bitch, please. As if I care.*

Yeah, I was petty, and that bastard needed to know his ass didn't live here anymore. If I couldn't step foot in his new place, he couldn't step foot in here.

"I had so much fun. Wait 'til I tell you where we went—" Suni started.

I cut her off, "Well, wait until I tell you about the surprise I have for you."

"Um…" Ryan started.

I turned to him. "What?" Then, I remembered my promise to myself. "I'm sorry, did you need to tell me something?" I asked with a forced, warm smile creasing my lips.

Ryan chuckled under his breath. "Naw, nothing that can't wait. I'll contact you later this week."

With my face frozen in perpetual sweetness, I said, "Okay, just call me." I imagined myself slamming the door in his face, but instead, I waited on him to turn away.

20

I made a conscious effort to quietly close the door. I then turned to Suni, feeling my heart expanding with love for her, I kissed her forehead, running my fingers through her braids.

"So, you had a good time with Daddy?" I struggled to let her go first before I told her about her newly painted walls. I took her by the hand, and we bounced up the stairs.

"We had so much fun—we went to Dave & Busters and I won all kinds of prizes. And then, I got to decorate my room over Daddy's and picked out my comforter and wallpaper in my new favorite color, lavender."

I stopped at the top stair. "Lavender? I thought pink was your favorite color?"

"Not anymore." She threw up her hand. "Here are some pictures." Suni took a dark purple cell phone from her pocket and started swiping.

"Where did you get an iPhone?" I felt dizzy.

"Mr. Gerald got it for me—see, this is the wallpaper." She continued to swipe through pictures.

"Who?"

"Look... Right here... This is my canopy bed and a flat screen on that other wall—see? In this picture there's my new rug with lavender, purple, and gold. You like it?" Her finger was swiping away.

"Yeah, that's cute—who is Mr. Gerald?" My head was still spinning a bit. Surely, it wasn't who I thought.

"You know... Daddy's—Oh! Oh! Look at my desk and computer—right here." Suni shoved the phone in my face. "Don't you love it?"

"It's really cute, baby." I didn't want to burst Suni's bubble so I, calmly as possible, shuffled through her pictures while questions swam through my head. I finally placed her bag on the floor as we continued to stand at the top of the stairs. I knelt in front of her and slipped her phone into the pocket of my sweat pants.

"Your dad was out of line getting you a cell phone without speaking to me first so I'm going to hold onto it until I can get in touch with him." I kissed her cheek, stood, and picked her bag up. "Now, for *my* surprise... Seeing as I thought your favorite color was pink, I painted your room." I pushed in the door and presented her new room like a game show host.

I wasn't sure if her mind was still on her phone resting in my pocket or she was simply not impressed with my redecorating efforts. "What do you think?"

Suni stepped in, looked around, and turned to me. "Can I have my phone for just a minute to call Daddy? He said it was okay for me to have it..." She was, at the very least, disinterested in her new, and obviously less-spectacular, room than the one at Ryan's home. Suni had never been a bratty girl but I feared this kind of shit would turn her into a monster—and in that moment, I hated Ryan for it.

I breathed in and out. One... Two... Three...

"I said I'll talk to him and—"

The corners of her mouth turned down and I saw her chest rising just before she interrupted me, "—Daddy didn't even give it to me. It was a present from Mr. Gerald," she spat out.

"Who?"

Suni's eyes were on my pocket and I knew it was killing her to not have her phone returned to her. A single tear escaped one of her large, deep-set eyes and my heart dissolved into a million pieces. "Mr. Gerald lives with Daddy... I think he's Daddy's husband."

After I answered every painstaking question from Suni about her father being gay, I slowly backed out of her bedroom, turned, and made my way down the hall. I slipped her iPhone into my top dresser drawer and made my way to my bathroom, turned on the shower, and undressed.

Chapter 3

RYAN

The bumper-to-bumper traffic on I-75 that made weekday commuting more torturous than toothpicks propped inside of eyelids, much to my chagrin, was non-existent the morning I brought Suni back to Melissa. In fact, the interstate was as placid as a lake on a chilly day. As counterintuitive as this may seem—that was a problem for me.

What I needed at that moment was chaos. I needed to be honked at and given the middle finger by an angry driver. The threat of my rear bumper being clipped by a teenager texting instead of watching the road needed to be real. Hell, even a second-too-long glance and wave from a man wearing a wedding band would have sufficed. Any distraction, big or small, would have been welcomed with open arms.

The tires on my new Mercedes were built for speed, so conquering the middle lane at an eighty mile an hour pace was child's play. I allowed my head to sink deeper into the headrest and turned the radio up louder, but my thoughts of Suni wouldn't be denied. Echoes of her melodic laugh drowned out the music blaring through my speakers. Her scent lingered in my nostrils. For the first time since my divorce, I felt my child would be better off living with me.

I sat in the car for a few minutes and tried to corral my emotions before entering our home, but Gerald's instincts are razor sharp. He can sense when I'm upset from a mile away. I needed to look strong, act strong, and sound strong. Unfortunately, I was none of those things. My eyes were moist with tears. My breathing was sporadic. My hands quaked. I opened the armrest and fished for my medicine. One prescribed panic pill left. I swallowed it and shut my eyes until my emotions quit swirling and order was restored.

Get it together, Ryan. You agreed to this joint custody arrangement. Suni needs her mother—even if she is a few sandwiches short of a picnic.

Gerald was in the kitchen doing the dishes when I entered.

"You okay?" he asked, not bothering to look at me.

"I'm fine."

"You took your medicine?"

"What makes you think I need to?"

"Because I know you." He dried off his hands and came over to me. "You've been crying."

"How can you tell?"

"I can see the moisture around your eyes and nostrils." He pointed to the living room. "Go sit down. We need to talk."

I did as I was told. I plopped down on the sofa and Gerald sat in the high-back chair a few feet away.

"What's wrong?" I asked.

"Nothing is wrong. I just want to talk about something that's been on my mind all weekend."

"Does it involve Suni?"

"Yes... indirectly. Mainly, it involves you."

"What did I do?"

26

"You referred to me as your husband."

"I always refer to you as my husband."

"I know that, but I'm not sure it was the best thing to say in front of Suni. You didn't even talk to me about it before you did it. Do you think that was wise?"

"I think that's reality. We agreed that you'd meet her this weekend."

"Meet her... not introduce me as your husband."

"You're making more out of that than you need to," I said and rolled my eyes.

"Maybe," Gerald replied in that calm but intense tone he uses when he's serious, "but that doesn't mean Melissa is going to be as nonchalant about it when she finds out."

"How is she going to find out about that?"

Gerald sighed and shook his head pitifully.

"Ryan, kids talk. Especially, kids Suni's age. They don't have filters. They say whatever comes into their minds. I'm not suggesting she's going to go back to her mom gossiping like some catty teenager, but at some point, Melissa is going to ask her about the weekend. And Suni's response is going to be unfiltered and—"

"Look, I agree that Suni may say something that could hurt her mother's feelings, but I can't live my life tiptoeing around Melissa's crazy moods. I introduced you as my husband. If Melissa finds out and starts feelin' some kind of way, I'll deal with her reaction. Truth be told, Melissa will probably be mad once Suni tells her about all the fun we had at Dave and Busters and IHOP—two places Melissa always hated."

"I'm through with it," Gerald said and threw up his hands. He pressed his index finger and thumb together and moved them from left to right across his lips to symbol zipping his mouth shut.

"Good," I said and moved within inches of his face. "Let me seal these lips with a kiss before you think of something else to say."

Monday morning's rays slithered through my bedroom blinds and caressed my face. My eyelids fluttered and remained open just enough for me to squint at the clock on my nightstand—7:06 a.m.

I yawned and stretched my arms until life surged back into my dead limbs. I ran my arm over Gerald's side of the bed, but I knew he wouldn't be there. He worked in Arlington, an hour away, so he'd been gone for an hour by the time I opened my eyes.

The consequences of being late for a mediation scheduled to start at nine was enough to motivate me to get out of bed. By the time the clock on my car's dashboard read 7:54, I was turning off Lemmon Avenue and merging onto busy I-75. During my four-mile trek on the busy interstate, I encountered the angry, distracted, and flirtatious commuters I longed to deal with the day before.

I swooped into the underground parking garage of the Century Building where the Troy Law Firm, my place of employment, was located. Luckily, my favorite parking spot was available. I grabbed my briefcase and the bagged lunch Gerald made for me and climbed out my car.

"Your husband!"

The words echoed like a voice in a cave. I froze. My head swiveled, but I didn't see anyone. A chill raced up my spine. I looked for the security guard that was supposed to be on duty, but as usual, he was nowhere to be found.

There'd been two muggings in the garage within a six-month period, so I had no desire to remain in that spot. I started to take another step, but my momentum was halted again by the haunting voice.

"Your fucking husband!"

This time the voice sounded closer.

A silhouette emerged from between two SUVs parked a few feet away from my car. The shadow materialized—it was Melissa.

"You introduced my child to your *fucking husband!*"

"Melissa," I said and took a deep breath, hoping it would settle my heart rate. "You scared the shit out of me. I thought you were a mugger."

"I should knock you upside your head the way a mugger would," Melissa said and walked toward me. "You know, I dealt with the humiliation that came my way when you came out of the closet. When you moved out of the house so you could be your *true self*, I didn't put up a fight. I swallowed my pride and let you go and do your *gay thing*. Now I have to hear from my daughter that you are living with the same motherfucker you cheated on me with. And to make matters worse, you're going around calling that pillow-biter your *husband*."

"Melissa, I understand you might be mad, but coming to my job with this mess ain't right. I've got a meeting to prepare for. We can talk about this tonight. I can call you around—"

I believe I offered a time that I would call Melissa, but the words must have gotten caught up in the wind current created by her slap. Stars appeared. My ears rang. Puddles of water formed in my eyes. My briefcase went left and my lunch bag flew right. I always thought it was just a figure of speech to say that someone got the *shit slapped out of them*, but at that moment, I became a believer. Melissa hit me so hard that I could feel my bowels move.

"Don't bother callin'... you sick bastard. The next time we talk, I'll be sitting next to my attorney." Melissa stabbed my forehead with her index finger and pushed my head back so hard that I staggered. "I'm taking your ass to court to get full custody."

My first instinct was to try to grab her by her weave, but the pain from her blow was debilitating. With my jaw smarting, I watched my ex-wife spin on her heels and move with cat-like quickness. She slithered between two cars, and with the blink of an eye, vanished just as quickly as she'd emerged.

Have you had something embarrassing happen to you in public and the first thing you wonder is whether someone saw it? That was me, hoping to God none of my co-workers were watching with their cell phones aimed at me.

I moved my head robotically from right to left. I didn't see anyone filming or hear any laughter so I fixed my clothes, grabbed my briefcase and lunch bag, and clutched my ass cheeks as I scurried toward the parking garage elevator so I wouldn't become the first guy to *literally* have the shit slapped out of him.

Chapter 4

MELISSA

The papers had been filed and should have been on their way to Ryan's office. I wished I could've been a fly on the wall when the server slapped them in his hands. I hate that I even warned him but if he thought I was playing about filing for custody, he was about to find out I wasn't.

Every time I pictured Ryan that day in my home, and then imagined my daughter walking in on the same scene, I lost my mind—literally. Once I found out he was married, I raced to my attorney. I wasn't sure why him being married made the difference, but it did. My hate for him rose to a new level. How dare he put a man—his lover—on the same level he'd once placed me. Why couldn't he have cheated on me with—and ultimately marry—a woman? That would be tolerable. That would be less humiliating. I'm sure I would've been angry, but I could've learned to live with him moving on with another woman. This, I could not stomach.

The crazy thing was, I never had any opinion on homosexuality. I was totally indifferent. I felt people should be free to live their own lives. If you were a woman who was in love with another woman—not my business. If you were a man in love with another man—not my business—until it impacted me personally. Even I would have never guessed I would respond to Ryan being gay the way I had.

"Any straight judge will be on my side, right?" I paced the floor of my attorney's office.

Norvelle Kates calmly sat at his desk, watching me. His office was in a new and contemporary building in West Plano. The gray and taupe color scheme, intended to be comforting, proved not to be the case for me. The walls were light with one dark accent wall and the carpet was speckled with small circles and triangles in an array of pale, nondescript colors with gray as the background. There were pictures of he, his wife, and kids posted all over the office. His expensive furniture, expansive liquor bar on one side and loaded coffee bar in the waiting area, was reflected in the bill for my divorce but he was worth every penny, so I didn't mind the amenities.

"Are you okay, Melissa?"

"I'm right, right? No judge is going to be okay with a man who inflicted such pain on me having joint custody of his daughter since he married the actual man I walked in on him with?"

"Look, you have every right to feel the way you do. But, honestly, now that same sex marriage is legal, there's no difference between this and if it had been a woman." Norvelle was a tall and fit brother transplanted in the Dallas area from Chicago. He was manly and sharp and was instantly empathetic to my dilemma when I initially contacted him explaining my husband was coming out of the closet. "However, I will do my best to make sure we present in front of a judge who may share our similar viewpoint. We have to be careful to not come off as homophobic. It gets tricky."

I landed in one spot for a moment, noticing the toes of both my Jimmy Choos rested between one circle and a triangle, and then I turned to him. "I'm not homophobic. I just don't want my daughter exposed to lascivious acts by her own father."

"Well, we should get a call in a few moments saying that he's been served. Once that happens, be prepared for a fight."

"We'll win, right? I'm right about that, right?" I was pacing again.

"You sure you're all right?" Norvelle now stood behind his desk.

"We have to make the judge feel my pain."

"Can I pour you a drink?" He made his way to the bar.

"I don't drink."

Norvelle handled one glass and poured himself a Vodka Tonic just as the phone rang. He carried his drink back to his desk and picked up the receiver.

I landed in a new spot matching the toe-pointed circle and triangle in front of me from before. I waited on him to deliver word. I kept my eyes on my toes but listened. I heard the phone land in its cradle.

"He's been served."

I stepped on the circle and triangle, and then made eye contact with Norvelle. "In three-two-one..."

My phone vibrated in my hand and I turned the screen towards Norvelle, showing him Ryan's name illuminated.

IGNORE.

It rang again. IGNORE.

And then, the text messages began. I swiped across my screen and read aloud.

DING. "So, this is where we are?"

DING. "So, this is how you wanna play it?"

DING. "You really want to keep my daughter away from me?"

DING. "Thanks for reminding me that you are the evil bitch I always knew you were."

DING. "You want a fight?"

DING. "OK get ready."

DING. "I'm—"

"That's enough. But let me know if he threatens you, physically, in any way. And keep all those messages. If nothing else, we can show he's harassing you so don't respond. We'll get a temporary order revoking his visitation, keeping him away from your daughter, and then we'll go to court to make it permanent." Norvelle downed his drink. "That's the plan, anyway."

I got back to the circle and the triangle on the other side of the office and exhaled. The taupe-colored circle and the lavender triangle were comforting but I couldn't stay there. "Okay, I need to get going so I can pick Suni up from school. I think I'll get her early, just in case." My silver Hermès Birkin bag knock off rested in the window seat just before I snatched it up and swiftly made my way out.

"Okay, keep me posted," were Norvelle's parting words.

"You know I will," I blurted out just before closing his door behind me.

Suni still had two hours of school left but I wanted to one up on Ryan just in case he tried picking her up. Just in case.

"Hi, I'm Suni Gray's mother and I need to get her early from school. It's her grandmother..." I said in my most sincere voice without really saying anything.

"Oh, I'm so sorry. Let me get her." The school secretary, a young redhead with hair down to her waist, dared not ask any questions. She held the phone's receiver on her shoulder and pointed to the computer at the kiosk. "Don't forget, you'll need to sign her out."

"Oh, right." I hoped I wasn't making Suni miss out on anything important because I felt strongly about her getting a good education. She was such a smart girl. But she worked hard and one afternoon off wouldn't hurt anything.

Suni came stumbling into the office holding her backpack, a textbook, and a jacket. She sat on the floor and stuffed her things in the opening of the vinyl bag. "What's wrong with Nanna?"

"Come on, let's go."

Suni was holding a paper in my direction. "I have a field trip on Friday. We're going to a museum and Missy said I could ride in the car with her and her mom."

"Okay, I'll take a look at it." I folded the paper and slid it into the pocket of my coat. "You're gonna need that jacket so take it back out." I turned to the secretary who was watching us closely. "Thank you so much."

"Um hm, sure..." She barely waved. "Bye, Suni."

We rushed through the doors and made our way to my waiting car up front. We got in and secured our seatbelts.

"What's wrong with Nanna?"

"Nothing. We're going to the movies." I watched through the rearview mirror as Suni gasped, and then laughed.

I wasn't ready to tell her she wouldn't be seeing her father for a while because I didn't want to ruin her good mood. She was too tickled to be playing hooky from school for me to spoil it for her with that tidbit of news.

We made our way to the theater, loaded up with popcorn and candy, and stumbled into the age-appropriate movie playing, already twenty minutes into its viewing. I could feel my phone vibrating in my pocket the whole time, but I ignored it. It couldn't be anyone but Ryan, and I loved the thought of him having a meltdown. I was the one known for psychotic breaks, so I wanted him to feel helpless for a change.

I'd taken many medications since being diagnosed, what my doctors called maintenance therapy, going through all kinds of side effects, sometimes getting better and sometimes not. Once I gained twenty pounds and found that to be more depressing than the disease itself. To add to it, there had been many bouts with suicidal thoughts. Although I'd never attempted it, I certainly battled with them.

Lithium worked well for my manic moods, but not only did it cause me constant nausea, it killed my sex drive. I couldn't have that. And it seemed there was always some side effect I just wasn't willing to live with, so I tried using my own mind control to ward off the highs and lows of bipolar depression. It was becoming increasingly more and more difficult, but I felt I was managing it all.

It had been three days and Suni and I hadn't left the house since the Tuesday I'd picked her up from school. I knew there was something wrong with that, but I just couldn't bring myself to get up and go to work—or get her to school. I told myself I was trying to prevent Ryan from kidnapping her but when I said it aloud, it sounded crazy. He wouldn't do that. But then, I told myself I couldn't take the risk.

I had turned off the ringer to my phone. The battery was even dead for hours before I knew it. I should've guessed it would alarm my mother, but I just wasn't thinking clearly. Or, maybe I wanted to alarm her. When she finally came over, using her key to come in, I wasn't surprised.

Suni had been trying to get me up and out of the house. I'd left her to feed and take care of herself—she'd done it before but this time I could see fear in her eyes when she prodded me, trying to get me out of bed. Sleep was all I could do. Trying to simply lift an arm seemed to be an impossible task. I knew it wasn't right putting her through that, but I really couldn't get it together.

My parents stood over me in my bedroom. I could see my mother talking on her phone, but my eyes were so heavy I couldn't tune into what was happening. At one point I heard her asking me to take a shower and that's when it dawned on me that I hadn't washed my body in days. I wanted to do what she asked but I couldn't move. I wanted to respond to her—I wanted to say something—anything. But no words would come out and neither could I make eye contact. Again, sleep was all I could do. I didn't want to sleep but I just couldn't wake up...

...but, when I did, a doctor was standing over me in an unfamiliar room and the smell of ammonia stung my nose. My parents had me committed. Again.

Chapter 5

RYAN

"**I** can't believe that bitch is trying to take my child."

I must've repeated that sentence one hundred times. Being served those papers stung more than the blow Melissa landed on my face a few days earlier.

"Spite—nothin' but spite. That's the only reason she would do something like this to me."

Rage clouded my vision, but I could still see the half-moon shaped ice cubes floating in my Courvoisier. I gripped the chiseled glass and closed my eyes while the expensive cognac sloshed in my mouth and snaked down my throat.

"It's gon' be all right, baby," Gerald said, his fingers sank deep into my shoulders.

Normally, his massages were the panacea to my stress, but a jackhammer wouldn't have penetrated the boulders in my shoulders.

"Your shoulders are hard as rocks. You should try to rest."

"She knows that keeping Suni from me is the one thing that will hurt me the most. I tried calling her, but she won't pick up the phone. And she's ignoring my texts. I went over there—"

"Even though I told you not to."

"I know you told me not to, but my frustration got the best of me. I needed to look that heifer in the face so I could ask her why she would take things this far. She didn't answer the door, but I know she was in there."

"Did you try to call Suni?"

"Yes, about five times. The first two times I called the phone just rang. I called a few times after that and it started going straight to voicemail. I know that wench took my baby's cell phone so I can't contact her. I called Suni's school. The director told me my baby hasn't been at school all week."

"Baby, Melissa is just—"

"An evil bitch," I barked. "And to add insult to injury, she had me served with papers at my fucking job." I smacked the table so hard I hurt my hand. "That fat fucker showed up in the lobby and served me in front of my boss. You should've seen the smug look on his face. It's like he was getting off on it."

"He probably was. How many chances does he get to serve an attorney? It probably made his day." Gerald rubbed my shoulders harder. "But, in her defense, she can't control the time and place the guy served you with papers."

"I know that Gerald. I'm just pissed this bitch would take it here. She's selfish and bitter... Always has been."

"Hurt people—hurt people," Gerald said, sounding as calm as Morgan Freeman narrating a story.

Gerald was always the calming force in our home. But as I sat there staring at court papers—my emotions swirling in my gut like a tornado—his self-control was as irritating as fingernails on a chalkboard. I wanted him to share my rage. I longed for him to grab his car keys and force me to hold him back so he couldn't go to Melissa's house and kick in the door. But that wasn't him. My Gerald was cool, calm, and collected— sometimes to a fault.

I guzzled the rest of my drink and grimaced as it sizzled going down.

"Well, if she wants to go to war, I'm ready to get dirty too."

"Calm down," Gerald said and patted my shoulders. He pulled out a chair and sat across from me at the kitchen table. "When you're angry, you tend to overreact. I want you to calm down, collect your thoughts, and *respond.*"

My eyes rolled harder than the dials inside of a slot machine. I wanted my co-pilot to be a hell-raiser, willing to go to jail for the cause. Not Yoda, spouting jewels of wisdom and discouraging retaliation.

"I'm sure there are some very good attorneys that specialize in family law at your firm," Gerald said.

"Yes. I think I'll reach out to Vincent."

"Who?"

"Vincent Malloy. You know, the tall, white guy I introduced you to at the Christmas party. The one who wouldn't put down the karaoke mic all night."

Gerald's face scrunched and shook his head. "Too goofy—hard to take serious. I'm sure he's good at what he does, but you need someone with a presence."

"White or black?"

"Doesn't matter, as long as the person commands the room when they're in it." Gerald wagged his finger. "But, I think it should be a woman representing you."

"Why?"

"Because a woman attacking another woman looks less like bullying and more like dissecting."

41

"Good point." I snapped my fingers. "I know just the person—Janice Mower."

"Is she good?"

"I'll put it like this, her last name is apropos. She mows down every attorney she faces in court. On top of that, she's a lesbian. She *gets* us."

"I've never heard you mention her."

"She's relatively new to the firm. Been there about four months. That's why I didn't think of her first, but we have a great rapport. She has a laid-back attitude, she's from California, but she's a pit bull in the courtroom. If her schedule is free, I'm sure she'll help us."

"Speaking of *us*," Gerald said. He reached across the table and cupped my hand with both of his hands. He squeezed and spoke in a tone that hovered just above a whisper. "There's something we need to discuss."

"What?"

I could feel his hands trembling. His bottom lip became lodged between his teeth. Those dreamy eyes of his filled with water. I placed my free hand on top of his.

"What's wrong?"

A rogue tear broke free and raced down Gerald's left cheek. He looked down at the table and said, "I don't want to be the cause of you losing your child." His voice cracked as if his throat was filled with the sands of the Sahara Desert. "I think it would be best if I moved out. I could move back to New York and stay with my brother until this all blows over."

I watched as the tear dangled from his chin and then fell to the table. The love of my life was crying because he didn't want to be a burden to me. I could feel my heart melting. Our hands melded together to form an anvil sized fist. Up until that point, we were united in spirit, but while fear swirled around our bodies as we sat at that kitchen table, I felt like Gerald and I had truly become one.

I pried my hand loose and gripped his chin, forcing him to look up at me.

"I'm only going to say this one time... we are a team. We sink or swim together. When I walk into Janice's office, you will be by my side. Whether I win or lose this case, I won't have to call you long distance to tell you the results because you'll be in the courtroom with me."

Gerald took a deep breath and unleashed a sigh of relief. After wiping away his tears, he looked at me and mouthed, *Thank you.* His pain became my pain. To know that he'd serve himself up as a sacrificial lamb let me know that my decision to leave Melissa for him—as off-putting as it may have been to some—was the right decision for me.

I offered a reassuring smile and said, "No... Thank you."

Janice Mower's eyes scanned from left to right, but her head didn't move while she studied the custody papers. She placed the document on her desk and stared at them. I wondered what type of visuals danced in her head. Was she thinking of a defense strategy? Was she considering declining to represent me? Hell, was she wondering what she'd eat for dinner that evening? She had the type of poker face that could win her a lot of money in Las Vegas.

Eventually, Janice's eyes found their way to mine. She leaned back in her chair and pushed away from the desk just enough to have room to drape one leg over the other.

"Do you want me to tell you what you *want* to hear or what you *need* to hear?"

I thought about her loaded question for a moment and replied, "Both."

"Good answer," Janice said, "because there is good and bad news. I like dealing with people who embrace both."

"I would think everyone would embrace good news."

"You'd be surprised. Some of the people I represent are born pessimists. Their negative energy shrouds them like a rain cloud. They blow off good news and practically plead for me to give them the 'catch'. They drain the life out of a room."

"Well, I'm not going to lie, this situation has soured my mood. But I promise, I'll try to keep my spirits up."

Janice nodded. "Okay, well here's the good news... you can win. The world is changing. Same sex marriages are legal in Texas." She uncrossed her legs, leaned forward, and planted her elbows on her desk. "But you have a few obstacles standing in your way. One, we're in conservative-ass Dallas, Texas. Some of the most sanctimonious people I've ever met live. Technically, same sex marriage may be legal here, but it's not necessarily *legal* in the court of public opinion. Texas isn't a part of the Bible Belt, but Texans sure have 'Bible Belt' tendencies—recite the gospel on Sundays and spend the rest of the week being intolerant of anyone who doesn't walk, talk, or act like them."

"Trust me, I know."

Janice continued, "The judges I've encountered here have those same tendencies. They are supposed to be unbiased and rule in accordance with the law, but they are cut from the same conservative cloth. I see them come up with bullshit ways to twist the law to fit their opinions like a tailored suit. Some of them will deal with their cases getting turned over in appeal before they rule in favor of something that goes against their raci..." Janice stopped short of letting the word fly and adjusted on the fly, "...I mean *conservative*, views."

"I understand," I replied.

"Secondly, you are now married to the person whom you cheated with. Your ex-wife is already a sympathetic figure."

I nodded in agreement and stared at the floor.

"You wanted me to tell you what you need to hear."

"I'm fine. Just processing what you've said."

"You've had joint custody since the divorce. Now she wants full custody. What happened?"

I shrugged.

Janice stood up and walked over to the small refrigerator a few feet away. She opened it and grabbed a bottle of water. "You want one?"

"No, thank you."

"Ryan, you're an attorney so I didn't want to give you this speech, but I see I have to." She shot me a parental, disappointing look. "If I'm going to represent you, I need to know exactly what I'm up against. That means, you can't leave anything out."

I felt like a child who'd brought home a bad report card. After clearing my throat, I said, "We were doing good. Sure, there has always been that post-divorce tension, but we were managing this new arrangement relatively well. And then..."

"What?"

"Last week, I had my daughter for the weekend. I introduced her to my husband."

"You kept your husband hidden from your daughter?"

"And her mother," I replied.

Janice cringed. "Ouch." She took another sip and sat down. "Let me guess, Melissa found out about your husband—the man she feels broke up her marriage—from your daughter?"

I nodded.

"Sloppy."

"In hindsight it was," I replied. "but you don't understand the type of woman I'm dealing with. Melissa is volatile. I feel guilty about everything that happened between us. Honestly, I didn't know how to talk to her about Gerald."

"That's understandable. But you were wrong for introducing your child—"

"Suni," I interjected.

"Suni," Janice repeated, and bobbed her head to acknowledge her inadvertent faux paus. "You should-n't have introduced..."

"Gerald," I said.

"Yes, Gerald... you shouldn't have introduced Gerald to Suni before you made Melissa aware of your new status."

"Guilty as charged."

"What happened when she found out?" Janice probed.

"She came to my job and attacked me," I flatly stated.

"What?"

"She attacked me," I repeated. "She walked up to me in the parking garage and smacked my face—hard."

"Did you hit her back?"

"No."

"Good. Did you call the police?"

"No."

"You should've." Janice pulled out a pad of paper and started writing notes feverishly. "Were there any witnesses to this assault?"

"Not that I know of. I realize now I should've called the police, but I didn't because I figured she'd let out her frustration and leave it at that. I had no idea she'd go to this extreme."

"Is Melissa always that aggressive?"

"When she's not on her meds."

Janice's eyebrows arched. There was a twinkle in her eyes. She leaned back in her seat, placed her hands on her stomach, and her intertwined fingertips.

"Tell me more."

"Melissa was diagnosed as being bipolar when we were in college. It started with an outburst in class and evolved into verbal attacks on professors. One night, I got a call from her roommate telling me Melissa went berserk because the girl drank some of Melissa's orange juice. Melissa beat the crap out of the girl and left the dorm wearing nothing but a t-shirt and panties. Campus police found her sitting on the lawn outside her dorms cradling that carton of juice in her arms like a baby and talking to herself."

Janice's fingers went to work again as she scribbled more notes. From where I sat, I could tell she was writing in shorthand. The paper looked like it was covered with hieroglyphics.

"Unfortunately, I'm going to have to cut this short," Janice said and glanced at her wristwatch. "I have a mediation to get to in an hour. Is there anything else you want to share?"

I shrugged and shook my head.

"Is there anything about your behavior I should know? Anything that can be used against you?"

Suddenly, time stood still. My thoughts raced back to the day Melissa caught me with Gerald—the incident that shattered my marriage. I regretted what happened. I regretted the way my actions destroyed an already fragile woman. Mostly, I hated the way discussing that night made me feel.

Janice and I engaged in a stare down for what seemed like a minute. She wanted to hear the truth. I wasn't prepared to tell her. With a straight face, I shook my head while saying, "I can't think of any-thing."

Chapter 6
MELISSA

I lost track of the days. It had been a long time since I'd found myself in this situation—locked in, restrained, and drugged. With all the chemicals designed to make me feel better flowing through my veins, I really didn't. I was keenly aware of the circumstances and what this setback meant with keeping custody of Suni. Ryan would be thrilled.

I was in and out, dozing off and on. Because I had no concept of time, it felt as if I had been alone for forever. When I heard the door opening, I wanted to be relieved. But I also knew that someone coming into the room wasn't necessarily a good thing.

It was a scrawny, pale faced man in a lab coat. I kept my eyes on him, waiting for him to speak. He was scrolling through an electronic tablet he held, swiping through screens before his eyes even landed on me. I couldn't read him because his expression was blank, and then, as if he were putting on an act, he smiled.

"Good afternoon, Melissa. I'm Doctor Steiner."

That was my first indication of the time of day. I would've guessed morning.

"How are you feeling?"

Afraid to answer the question, I simply inhaled deeply and exhaled slowly.

"I hear you had a pretty good night last night, but you slept through breakfast." He touched my bound hand with his own. "You must be hungry, so let's get you something to eat."

"How long have I been here?" I managed to ask through a desert-dry throat.

"You arrived—" He swiped through his tablet. "—last Saturday."

"What's today?" I moved to sit up but discovered it was impossible to do. The straps on both wrists kept me immobile.

"It's Tuesday," he mumbled.

"I've been here a week?"

"Actually, over a week."

I couldn't believe it. "A whole ten days?" I felt tears burn my eyes. Damn it. Frustration was building up inside me. "Where's my daughter—where's Suni?"

"Your daughter is with your folks. She's fine."

"When can I get out of here?" The tears rolled and there was nothing I could do to stop them.

Dr. Steiner pulled open the blinds, letting in a blinding light. The warmth felt good but for only a second.

"Let's take things one step at a time. You had a good night so we're going to remove the restraints today and we'll see where that takes us. If things go along smoothly, maybe next week you can go home."

A soft whimper came from my throat.

"It's fine, Melissa. Your parents are stopping by today so why don't you have some lunch, rest, and we'll get you cleaned up for your visit."

A younger man stepped in the room behind Dr. Steiner and stood next to my bed. Dr. Steiner nodded and the nurse unlocked the straps from my hands, using a key.

Immediately, I rubbed my reddened and sore skin. I wanted to reflect on the week I had lost but I knew I needed to not think about it at that moment. The focus was to get better so I could get out. And, if it wasn't too late, I needed to do it before Ryan knew where I was. That was the real goal.

"Thank you. That's better." I wiggled my fingers and rotated my wrists. I sat up in the bed and finger-combed my hair. I could feel it standing up all over my head. I knew I must've been a sight.

"Your lunch is on its way." Dr. Steiner still held what I felt was a fake smile on his face, but his tone was surprisingly soothing.

"Good. I'm really hungry." I wasn't at all, but I knew doctors liked to hear shit like that. I would force myself to eat everything they fed me no matter what it was because I knew, for them, it was a sign of being healthy.

"Here we go." Dr. Steiner stepped back, making room for the young lady bringing my tray. "Let's get some food in you. You don't have to eat all of this but eat what you can."

The hospital worker placed the tray on the table and wheeled it in front of me. She pulled off the cover plate, revealing spaghetti and meatballs and a small garden salad. I hated hospital food and I hated spaghetti and meatballs, but I dug right in, pretending it was steak and lobster.

"Good girl," Dr. Steiner said and then patted my shoulder. "Someone will be in to help you bathe in an hour or so. We want you presentable for your parents when they get here."

"Is Suni coming with them?" I asked between chews.

"You don't think that's a good idea, do you—her seeing you like this?"

I peered up from my lunch and answered, "I guess not."

"If all goes well, like I said, you'll be home soon enough."

Dr. Steiner turned and followed the others out the room, leaving me alone. I knew from before that there was a camera, and I was under constant surveillance. I continued to eat until all the food was gone. I opened the small can of soda and poured it over the ice and leaned back in the bed. My eyes were so heavy, as much as I tried, I couldn't keep them open. I resented the drugs they kept pumped in my veins, but it was all a part of the game I had to play. My eyes closed.

Even though I had no appetite, eating that bland food did make me feel better. A shower and getting my hair brushed and braided by one of the nurses sent me back into a deep sleep. I slept so well that I thought I'd missed my parents coming to see me. Just as panic set in, the door opened.

"Oh, you're up. How did you sleep, Melissa?" A nurse named Ruby who had bathed me earlier and shampooed my hair was standing in the doorway.

Instead of answering her, I simply yawned and stretched.

"I hope you're up for visitors. Your mom and dad are here."

I sat up and swung my feet over the side of the bed. "I thought I missed them." I ran a hand over my braided hair.

"I'll go get them." She patted my knee. "You look just fine, sweetie."

Every time I ended up in a place like this, I felt as if I'd let Mama and Daddy down. For so many years it seemed I had my life together and on the right track. I was a wife and mother with a promising career—a career I landed actually using the degree they'd sacrificed and paid for. They were once so proud of me and I knew they loved me—the reason they kept showing up time and time again when I broke away from reality. They loved me but I didn't know if the love was deeper than the disappointment. And if it was deeper, how long would it remain that way?

I tried putting a pleasant expression on my face but not having a mirror left me unsure of how I would appear to them. So, I wanted to focus on my conversation. My goal was to ensure them I was fine and would be coming home to care for my daughter myself.

Mama came through the door first. Slowly, she made her way to me.

I smiled but could tell only one side of my mouth joined in. "Hey, Ma."

"Sweetie... How are you feeling?"

My face felt twisted, so I readjusted my position on the edge of the bed, planning to stand to my feet to show that I was fine but wasn't sure if I was strong enough. I changed my mind and leaned back. "Good... Good. I don't even know why I'm here."

Just then, Daddy opened the door. He came to me faster than Mama had. He held me in his arms, kissing the top of my head.

"How you doin', kitten?" his voice was soothing.

"I'm better, Daddy. Feeling pretty good." I pulled back from his embrace. "I can't believe how long I've been here—a whole week."

"Don't worry about that." He took a seat next to Mama, just next to my bed.

I wanted to relax but I remained alert. "How's my baby?" I asked them.

"She's fine, of course. Missing you," my mother answered.

"What time is it? Is she still at school?" I looked around for a clock and realized there wasn't one. Nor was there a television.

"Um... Yes... She's at school," Daddy stumbled over his words.

"Well, what time is it?"

Daddy held up his wrist and then turned to Mama before he answered me. "It's three-thirty now."

"Shouldn't you guys be headed there to pick her up?"

"That's what we wanted to talk to you about, sweetie," Mama started.

"What's wrong?"

"Honey, the judge—" Daddy cut in, and then leaned forward. "The judge granted—Ryan found out you were—the judge is allowing him to get Suni today—he's picking her up today for a visit."

"No," I yelled. "How did you let this happen?" Tears burned my eyes.

"Baby, we tried to keep him from finding out but..." Mama's voice trailed off. "I think he may have called your office..."

"Don't let this happen, Daddy," I pleaded.

"Honey, it's going to be fine. It's just a visit—for now..." Daddy responded.

"Ryan's a good man," Mama said. "He'll do the right thing by Suni."

"That's not the point—I don't want her around that man." Tears were flowing freely now. "I hate Ryan for this—now he's going to keep her from me."

"That's not going to happen. I assure you. We'll do whatever we can to see to it," Daddy tried to reassure me.

"She'll be back with us next week. Don't worry—just work on getting better."

Once the tears turned on, I couldn't stop them. I wanted to address everything they said but I couldn't utter a word. I buried my head into my pillow and wailed. As badly as I wanted to stop crying, I couldn't. What felt like my father's hand was caressing my back. Desperation ran deep inside me and I imagined never seeing my baby again. Hopelessness seemed to whirl around me.

This was the end for me, and I imagined the relief on Ryan's face and the glee he must have felt. I was no longer a factor. I could see him jumping for joy and getting pleasure out of me having yet another nervous breakdown. I was a mess. I then second guessed why any man would want me—thinking it made perfect sense that Ryan would turn to someone else—man or woman. I was unlovable. A person that didn't deserve to live.

Chapter 7
RYAN

I can count on one hand the number of times I've been happy enough to scream: the day Suni was born; the day I got accepted into SMU's Law School; the day I passed the bar exam; and the first time I was able to hold Gerald's hand in public. When I showed up to court, I was prepared to go to war. Flanked by my attorney and Gerald, I relished the opportunity to face Melissa in court. Honestly, I was a bit let down when I learned that Melissa had been admitted to the hospital for psychiatric observation. The disappointment was temporary. The moment I realized how her absence impacted my case, that day in court catapulted to the top of my "scream" list.

You may have noticed that I left two seminal dates off my "scream" list—the day I decided to marry Melissa and the day I "came out" to my parents. Well, there is a simple explanation for that—those were two of the worst days of my life.

What's most interesting about the day I decided to marry Melissa and the day I told my parents I was gay, is that the two events happened simultaneously.

Woven together tighter than the patterns in your grandmother's favorite knitted blanket.

The year was 2011—Thanksgiving Day. Melissa and I discovered she was pregnant the day before, after she'd pissed on a half-dozen pregnancy sticks. We figured it would be awesome to tell our parents the next day. Well, *Melissa* thought it would be a fantastic idea. All she ever talked about was having a baby. She was supposed to be on birth control, but somehow, she *miraculously* got pregnant. That's an entirely different can of worms that I won't open at this moment. But I'll put it like this—I often questioned whether she suffered from selective amnesia when it was time for her to take her birth control pills.

I had misgivings about becoming a father. Melissa and I weren't married at that time. I was just getting started in my law career and wasn't making much money. And most importantly, I wrestled with my sexuality. So, bringing a child into the world at that moment seemed like the worst thing to do.

Melissa's parents, Guy and Elizabeth Carter, were two of the nicest people I'd ever met. Their reaction to the news was no surprise to me. We were huddled around their dining table eating Thanksgiving dinner when Melissa blurted out the news. She didn't give me a heads up before she did it; so, when I heard the announcement, I froze. My fork, which was covered with a mound of oyster dressing and cranberry sauce, was perched inches away from my lips.

Silence reigned as Melissa's words hovered over the table like morning fog. But, once those words slithered into her parent's ears, there was an eruption more powerful than the ash-spewing belch from Mount Vesuvius. Her parents wailed like revelers at Mardi Gras. I instantly became their favorite person; the man who'd fathered their first grandchild.

We spent the next two hours rejoicing with Melissa's parents. By the time we were preparing to leave and head over to my parent's home, The Carter's had called most of the people in their extended family and were already planning the baby shower.

Juxtapose the Carter's reaction to that of my parents, and you can understand why we felt like we'd stepped out of the Soul Train studios and into a Catholic Sunday service.

My parents, Lester and Claudia Gray, were hands down the most conservative black folk I've ever known. My dad was a card-carrying NRA member. My mother preferred to get her hair done by white stylists at John Jay Salon in a mall forty-five minutes away rather than at Ms. Sheila's Beauty Shop, the hair and nail salon that sat on the corner of their block. A beacon of entrepreneurial hope for all black folk in our neighborhood to see.

It probably wouldn't surprise you to know that my parents voted Republican. They even tried to convince me that Donald Trump's questioning of President Obama's citizenship was based on cogent evidence.

As we sat at a massive dining table, surrounded by eight chairs more than were ever needed, the news of Melissa's pregnancy landed with a thud.

"Hurry up and finish your dinner, Ryan," my mother said and stood up. She put on oven mitts and grabbed a pie from off the stove top. Walking like a mother carrying a sleeping newborn, she gently placed the pie in the center of the table and looked at it with admiration. "I can't wait for you to try my new pumpkin pie recipe."

That's right, she said pumpkin pie, not sweet potato pie. Another indication that my parents were the *whitest* black people walking the face of the earth.

"Uh-um," Melissa grunted.

I'd already been caught off guard at Melissa's parent's house, so I wasn't about to let it happen again.

"I got this," I whispered to Melissa and held her hand. "Momma... Dad. We have some news." I could feel Melissa's hand trembling. I squeezed tighter and allowed the deep breath I'd exhaled to escape my mouth slowly. With what little poise I could muster, I stumbled through the words, "We're having a baby."

The legs of my father's chair screeched so hard on the hardwood floors that I could envision the wood shavings left behind. He stood and pointed at me. "You. My bedroom. Now."

The command boomed like Darth Vader had issued it. All my father needed was a black mask, cape, and menacing theme music as he marched like a Drill Sergeant toward the bedroom.

My mother sprang from her seat and scurried behind him with the timidity of an 18th century geisha, minus the kimono and white makeup.

"Aww shit," I mumbled.

"You want me to come with you?" Melissa asked.

I could tell by the way she asked that she didn't mean it. Her offer to accompany me into the lion's den was as fake as that hairpiece Steve Harvey wore in the 90s.

"No. I've gotta deal with this by myself."

When I opened the bedroom door, my mother grabbed me by the forearm and pulled me in. "Ryan, what were you thinking?"

"He wasn't thinking," my father said.

Ever since I was a child, my mother fidgeted when she became nervous. She ran her hand across my left shoulder, smoothing out wrinkles that didn't exist and flicking away imagined pieces of lint. "You just became a lawyer, honey. This is going to derail your career."

60

She withdrew her hand as if she'd pricked a finger on one of those imagined wrinkles and cuffed her mouth. "What will my friends think?"

"They're going to think he made a mistake, sure enough. But they will realize that he's an honorable young man." My dad stabbed me in the chest with his index finger. "Because you're going to marry that girl. No son of mine is going to father a bastard."

Like the feeble flames that appear in a fireplace once charred wood is fondled by the tip of a hot poker, my father's finger jabs stoked a rage inside of me that had been dormant for years. I opened my mouth and spewed a retort so scorching that it made my parents reel.

"I'm not marrying anyone."

"Like hell you aren't," my dad said. "I didn't raise you to run from your responsibilities."

"I'm not running from my responsibility, but I'm not going to marry her."

My mother placed her hand on my cheek and caressed it. "Why won't you do the right thing and marry her, honey?"

"I'm not marrying her because—"

"Because of what, boy?" Dad said. "Spit it out."

"I'm gay."

Separately, those two words were far from formidable, but when coupled, they struck with the force of a tsunami.

My dad placed his hand over his heart and staggered. I couldn't tell if he was about to pledge allegiance to the flag or do his best Fred Sanford impersonation.

My mother's response wasn't so subtle. Apparently, my announcement obstructed the flow of blood to her brain. Like a drama school dropout starring in a low budget movie, she placed the back of her hand on her forehead, let out an awkward squeal, and fell to the floor.

"Dammit, Ryan. Why you wanna go and say something crazy like that? You made your mama faint."

We both knelt to pick her up and placed her on the edge of the bed. My dad sat next to her. I knelt at her feet.

My mother looked at me groggily. "Honey, did I... did I... hear you say—"

"Yes, Mama, you heard correctly... I'm gay. I've known for years. I've been fighting it, but I can't anymore. I was going to tell Melissa a week ago, but I couldn't find the nerve." The weight of the discussion forced my eyes downward. I stared at my feet while talking. "And then we found out yesterday she was pregnant. So, I don't feel right springing this on her. I'm going to keep it under wraps for now, but at some point, I'm going to tell her about my boyfriend... Gerald."

The whites of my mother's eyes appeared. Her head flopped backward and her upper body followed. She passed out again, but this time on the bed.

"Dammit, Ryan. Stop saying that shit." My father placed a few pillows under her head and looked at me. Flames flickered in his eyes. "Let me tell you something," he said through pressed lips and stood up. "You're going to marry her."

I stood. Our noses were less than six inches apart.

"Dad, I can't marry—"

"Shut up... you little faggot." He inched so close I could smell the turkey on his breath. "I will not let you embarrass this family. You're gonna keep that rainbow flag-waving shit in the closet. You're going to marry Melissa before that baby is born. And we're going to pretend you never told us about your little gay feelings."

"And if I don't marry her or hide my true identity?"

"That automatic draft that comes out of my checking account every month to cover your law school tuition will be stopped immediately. That car you drive—that's technically in my name—will be repossessed by this time next week." He leaned in. "And that million-dollar life insurance policy that has you listed as the beneficiary, will be changed. I'll leave the money to your mother's drunk-ass brother before I leave it to a twinkle toes son who brings shame to our family name."

Fifty-two thousand, six hundred, and forty-seven dollars—that's how much money I owed to SMU for Law School. Eighteen thousand, nine hundred, and ten dollars—that was the remaining balance on the BMW I drove. Forty-two thousand dollars a year—that's how much I earned as a junior attorney, fresh out of law school. There was no way I could afford to assume the tuition bill, car note, and care for my new baby off what I earned. So, I did what any smart person would do... I shut the fuck up.

"Are we clear?"

His words pierced my chest, plowed through my rib cage, gripped my heart, and yanked it out my body.

I nodded and swallowed hard. "Yes."

"Yes, what?"

"Sir."

Melissa and I got married five months later. Two months after that, my parents were killed in a car accident. The law school tuition payments became mine. The BMW payment became mine. That million-dollar life insurance policy that my dad used as a weapon to beat me into submission—never existed. He *forgot* to mention the policy lacked a necessary zero to make it worth one million.

I blew through that one-hundred thousand dollars faster than a fat kid holding a cheeseburger. After I paid for their funerals, back taxes, and a new, less expensive car in my name, I had just enough money to use as a down payment for our first home.

A new baby. A new bride. A new house. An old secret.

The courthouse steps looked like Grand Central Station at the end of the workday. Swarms of people moving around, oblivious to everything around them that didn't pertain to their cases. Some flashed that smile that only a winner can know. While others cursed, cried, and pointed accusatory fingers at briefcase holding attorneys who failed to earn their money.

Janice strutted like a stripper surrounded by a room full of losers on payday. She wore her confidence like a tattoo. Bold. Non-apologetic. The ideal person to combat an ex-wife with an agenda.

"That was easier than I expected," Janice said as we exited the courtroom and stood outside on the steps. "As long as she's battling mental health issues, and you don't do anything that will get you arrested, you should keep the custodial upper hand."

"What now?" Gerald asked. "Do we go and pick her up?"

"Yep," Janice replied. "I'm not going to get involved in all of that. She's with her grandparents now. Ryan, exercise extreme care when getting her from them. Remember what I said... don't do anything that will get you arrested."

"That's no problem. I still have a great relationship with her parents. They won't give me any problems."

Gerald and I shook Janice's hand. While she descended the courthouse steps, he and I engaged in a hug fit for the day's victory.

I drove straight to Melissa's parent's house and picked up Suni. Fortunately, Mrs. Carter—whom I call Miss Liz—had already packed my baby's suitcase.

As I grabbed Suni's things and we parted ways, Miss Liz hugged me and whispered in my ear, "This is for the best...at least until Melissa gets better."

Yes, this is what's best, but it's not temporary, I thought. *I intend to keep Suni until she graduated high school.*

"I agree, Miss Liz. While Melissa is dealing with her problems, living with me is the best thing for Suni. Don't worry, you guys can see her whenever you want."

"I know," said Miss Liz, fighting back tears.

Mr. Carter, who insisted I call him Mr. Guy the day we first met, stood there looking rock solid. "You run along," he said, and placed his arm around his wife's waist as a show of support. "And don't worry about talking to Melissa, we'll break the news to her."

By the time we made it back to the car, the trunk was open. Suni sat in the back seat looking somewhat confused by it all.

"I'll drive," Gerald said.

"Go, go," I said, gesturing for him to speed away as I buckled myself into the passenger seat. "I wanna get out of here before they change their minds."

"No need to speed off," Gerald whispered. "It will only upset her." He started the car and put it into gear. "Besides, a judge has ruled." He glanced back at Suni and smiled. "Baby girl is coming home with us."

Chapter 8

MELISSA

Every new week turned into one more week until I had been at Plano Presbyterian for a whole month. Yes, I was frustrated and every time I showed it, more days were added to my stay. My last week there was when Daddy confessed that Suni had been with Ryan all that time.

I wanted to tear some shit up in that place; instead, I held it together and told Daddy I understood. He kept insisting that Ryan wasn't trying to keep Suni from them or me. But I knew that fool better than they did. Anybody that could pretend—and pretend well—that he was into women, could fake anything.

For the longest I had tried to keep them from knowing the low-down dirty dog Ryan was, even when I had to tell them we were divorcing. It took me forever to tell them he was gay, but I never told them how I discovered it.

Once I saw how my parents reacted to the divorce, I knew they couldn't handle the whole truth. My father loved Ryan like a son and when Mr. and Mrs. Gray died, my father told him he was. "You're the son I never had," is how he put it. So, for the longest, I let my parents think we were just incompatible, going through a standard divorce. It wasn't until they kept pressing for us to go to counseling for Suni's sake that I had to tell them about his homosexual lifestyle.

My parents were speechless. They loved Ryan but made it clear that their loyalties were with me. They didn't hate him, but they hated the pain he'd caused me. Even though I was their daughter, it was as if their own son was coming out. They were disappointed but loved him anyway.

I didn't come from a homophobic family. There were several aunts, uncles, and cousins on both sides who were gay. Not much was ever said about it one way or another, so I reconciled that Ryan being gay wasn't the issue I was having with him. It was the deception. What he didn't understand was that if he had told me he was gay when we first found out I was pregnant; we could've remained friends and co-parented our daughter. We were friends. That's how things started out with us before casually turning into friends with benefits. It wasn't until after we were married and had Suni that I discovered my love for him. We were comfortable in our careers, doing our thing, with the appearance of a power couple and perfect family. He waited until I was good and settled into my happily ever after when he snatched the rug from beneath me. And for that, I'll forever hate him.

Ryan and I met at a mutual friend's barbeque. By chance, we were paired together in a game of Spades and quickly became shit-talking teammates and friends. We liked each other right away. It was amazing how we learned to read each other's body language and expressions even though we'd just met. We played all day, crushing everybody that came along. By the time the day was coming to an end, we were like old friends.

"You're cool," Ryan said to me, handing me a plate of ribs and potato salad.

"Thanks." I sat the plate on a nearby table and began shedding my shorts and tank top.

"Hey..." He stopped in his tracks.

"You know, nobody's gotten in this pool all day," I announced.

"What are you doing?" he asked, looking alarmed.

"Taking a swim before I eat all that food." I was down to my bikini and headed toward the pool.

"Oh, you're *that* chick." He smiled and appeared relieved.

"You coming?"

He snatched his shirt over his head and slipped off his vans. "You're not like the rest of these sistas here, afraid to get your hair wet."

I was already diving in the pool.

As the sun was setting, we chased each other around in the water, flirting and touching. I rode on his back, he held my legs; we were comfortable in a way I hadn't been with any other man.

I liked what I saw. Ryan wasn't the type I usually went for. He was taller than me, but not as tall as I liked. He was barely brown, and I certainly liked my man good and black. His body was unexpectedly chiseled and based on his conversation, I could tell he was brainy. He wasn't my kind of sexy, but he was still sexy, and I was eager to try something different. There was no way I saw love in our future, but I wanted to sample that tight body.

"You're cute," I told him.

Ryan blushed and said, "So are you."

We stared at each other for a moment and then went back to horse playing in the water—dunking each other's heads playfully. Finally, we dried off, ate our food, and said goodnight, leaving with the friends we'd each come with.

Nothing happened that day but when he called the next day and asked me out, I had every intention to sample the goods. When he resisted after that first dinner and movie, I thought he was trying to respect me. Looking back, I wonder something else now. But, ultimately, it didn't take long before we were all over each other and sex was a regular activity between us. I never thought once that he was attracted to anyone but me—woman or man.

It was that one slip up—one night of heated lust, I'd end up pregnant. It happened when one overnight trip to Ryan's turned into two. I hadn't packed my pills. In fact, I hadn't packed anything because I hadn't planned to spend the night—let alone the weekend. It was Sunday afternoon when I realized I was behind on my pill taking. *How could one missed day make a difference?*

Well, we found out six weeks later that it had.

I sat in the back seat of Daddy's S-Class Mercedes peering out the window. I was so busy still trying to comply so they didn't turn the car around, taking me back to medical prison, that I didn't notice the direction we were moving. Every emotion a person could name and feel was rumbling inside me even though those same emotions were chemically subdued. I just rode, sitting quietly and staring blankly.

"Your father and I thought for the first few days, you could stay with us. We made your old room up for you," my mother said, speaking over the smooth jazz coming from the speakers. "We've been checking on things at the house and everything's fine. Those nice neighbors you have to the west of you are keeping an eye out and collecting the mail. And we already picked up some clothes for you." She finally turned to face me. "Did you hear me?"

"When can I see Suni?" was my response.

"Ryan said he'd be bringing her to spend the weekend with us," Daddy spoke up.

"And y'all believe that?"

"Why wouldn't we?" he asked.

"Because he's a lying, low-down, dirty dog, that's why."

"Melissa, don't get worked up," my mother said. "He'll keep his word."

"Mama please, you told me two weeks ago that he was letting you bring her to see me. What about that?"

"That was different. He just didn't want her to see you in the hospital, that's all. He thought it might upset her and I think he was right."

"He could've at least let me talk to her on the phone after all this time." Tears burned my eyes. "He's trying to drive me to do something that will work against me. I know him."

"Then, don't give him what he wants, if that's true." Daddy turned the corner, and then into the driveway. Once the garage door opened, he drove forward slowly pulling in next to Mama's SUV.

I exhaled, grabbed a plastic bag full of my belongings, and unlatched my seatbelt. I wanted to go home so badly but I'd learned that fighting against the system didn't work. I would pretend to be satisfied being there so I could get home quickly, and then slowly back to my life. I only had a few more weeks of medical leave from work and going back on the job would ensure my chances of getting Suni.

"I made a pot roast and chocolate cake," my mother said. "Thought you'd like that." When all else failed, she solved every problem in the kitchen.

I could smell the food as soon as we stepped through the back door and into the kitchen. The aromas greeting us made me nauseous, but I dared not say a word. I would eat and pretend to enjoy it.

"Thanks, Mama. First, I want to shower and change, maybe even take a nap. Okay?"

"That's fine. You can eat later." The disappointment on her face struck me.

"You know, maybe I'll eat first. I haven't had your pot roast in forever."

Daddy and I sat at the table while Mama warmed up the food. There was an awkward silence, but we all pretended not to notice. Mama and Daddy robotically talked about the neighbors and the lawn service while I sat, numbly listening.

"I appreciate y'all..." my voice cracked with me being overcome with gratitude. "I realize how fortunate I am. Especially after seeing so many patients at the hospital all alone—no family to look out after them."

Daddy stood and kissed me on the forehead just as Mama placed a hot plate of gravy-covered roast, potatoes, and carrots, and a spinach salad in front of me.

"Everything is going to work out fine. You'll see," she offered.

"Your mother's right. You and Ryan can work this out. Everything doesn't have to be a fight." He added, "He'll do the right thing, just watch."

My parents pampered me and fielded calls from friends and family concerned with my well-being. I wasn't ready to see anyone except my daughter. She was the only one I was eager to talk to. I rested and ate for four days straight—hot breakfasts, cold lunches, and huge dinners. Cold breakfasts, hot lunches, and still huge dinners. All of it sprinkled with appetizers of

Lithium and other mood stabilizers. Between the food and the medication, I was gaining weight rapidly. I hated the added pounds, but it felt good being at my parents' home and I was getting back to myself—slower than I wanted, but I was getting there.

Mama and Daddy had lulled me into complacency and a false sense of security, believing that all would be well, and then the weekend came and went with no Ryan and no Suni. No returned phone call from him, no response to my text messages, no email or even a smoke signal. Nothing. I felt so helpless and hopeless.

God, kill him and that faggot he lives with.

Chapter 9

RYAN

Gerald's eyes burned holes into that tiny space between my eyebrows just above the bridge of my nose. He tried to make me look at him, but I wouldn't bite. We all learn at an early age to avoid staring into a predator's eyes unless you're ready to fight. At that moment, Gerald was a bighorn ram ready to lock horns. Rather than start a fight I knew I wasn't prepared to finish; I focused my attention on Suni—monitoring the way she tried to hide her green peas under the slice of bread on her plate.

"Suni," I said sternly, displaced aggression at its finest, "I see you hiding your peas under that bread."

Like any 8-year-old, the art of deception was foreign to her. Their trickery is uncovered by their clumsiness or their guilty body language—Suni was guilty of both. Without attempting to lie, she removed the bread and unveiled the uneaten peas.

"Do you remember what I said? No dessert if you don't eat your peas."

Suni slouched in her seat, crossed her arms, and stuck out her bottom lip. I was not moved by her silent protest, but Gerald was.

"How 'bout this," Gerald whispered as he leaned in close to Suni, "if you eat two scoops of those peas, I'll let you have some ice cream and you can watch whatever you want in our bedroom on the big television."

Like pixie dust, Gerald's words floated into Suni's ear and brought her slouched body to life. Her posture became as erect as a thirsty flower dowsed with water. She grabbed her spoon and used it like a landscaper planting a tree. The peas vanished.

"That's my girl," Gerald said and winked at her.

Suni smiled. Their bond was growing. With each passing day, I could see her gravitating to him. I wasn't sure how I felt about it.

"You're spoiling her," I said, still avoiding eye contact.

"Somebody's got to."

"What does that mean?"

Gerald put his knife and fork down and dismissed Suni with a slight head nod. The girl wasted no time getting up from the table.

"I'll tell you what I mean when you make eye contact with me while we talk."

I was the attorney, but Gerald was a much better debater. I'd often told him he would've made an awesome trial lawyer, but as a *Trust Fund Baby*, he never had to ponder a career. He had the luxury of working jobs until he tired of them. I often wondered if he admired or pitied me; a man who slaved through law school with the hopes that the title "Esquire" would bring about a prestige and freedom that people like Gerald are born with.

As much as I hated to admit it, I dreaded arguing with Gerald. He often made me feel like a mental midget, taking my words and twisting them. I could see the joy in his eyes as he pelted me with words that made me tilt my head slightly like a dog struggling to understand his owner's command. The passive-aggressive approach was the only way I ever got my way because verbal jousting with him was about as futile as tits on a bull.

I continued to carve my steak and chewed without looking up. I wasn't trying to be disrespectful, but I needed to stall while I figured out a clever comeback. My bucket of slick retorts was emptier than a crackhead's bank account.

I peeked at his plate and could see that Gerald hadn't lifted his silverware. He was itching for a fight, and whether I wanted to or not, squaring off with him was inevitable. I just hoped I could last three rounds.

"Okay," I said and exaggerated my sigh as I placed my knife and fork on my plate. "I'll play your little game." I put my elbows on the table and interlocked my fingers just under my chin. I know that was a corny display of machismo, but it was the most patronizing gesture I could come up with at that moment. "What did that last remark mean?"

"First, let me say thank you for looking at me while we speak. I know you place as much emphasis on courtesy and respect as I do."

Ouch. That jab landed square on my chin. Round One goes to Gerald.

"What I meant by that remark is," he continued, "you haven't been spending as much time with her as I have. As a result, she tends to gravitate to me more. That doesn't mean she loves me more; it just means she has a greater comfort level with me at this point. That's a *you* problem." Gerald shot a stiff finger in my direction and then turned it on himself. "Not a *me* problem."

"Umm, I work."

"So do I, but I make time. So do a lot of fathers out there, but they make time for their kids."

"A lot of fathers out there don't have the type of job I have."

"Oh, I forgot, you're Mr. Big Time Attorney. Your job is way more complex and important than most fathers out there."

I don't know if it was my ego or if I really believed what I said next, but before my brain could send the order to my lips to slam shut, a regrettable response spilled from my mouth.

"Yes," I said smugly, "my job *is* more complex and important than the jobs that most fathers have."

Before every thunderstorm, there is a climate change. Swirling winds. Rising tides. Darkening skies. Mother Nature's way of letting you know that something wicked is coming. Mother Nature wasn't a guest at our table, but make no mistake about it, I knew a storm was coming because the climate in that room changed.

It started with Gerald's posture. He adjusted his body and removed his elbows from the table. The back of his head kissed the chair, giving him a more relaxed look. His left eyebrow arched like the McDonald's logo. He placed his right hand on his thigh while his left fingers strummed the table. Those beautiful lips of his pursed and twitched moments before his pointed remark broke free.

"President Obama graduated magna cum laude from Harvard Law School. He taught law at the University of Chicago and went on to become a two-term President of the United States of America. Yet, he found time to be a hands-on father to two daughters. You think he was a little busy at times? Do you think your work schedule is any busier than his was while he spent hours teaching and helping students in law school?" Gerald's fingers became unified, and his strumming stopped with a synchronized four-finger table tap. "Do you think the responsibilities of your job are weightier than running the most powerful country in the world? President Obama found time to make sure Malia and Sasha were getting the fatherly attention they needed. Why can't you find a way to spend time with your *one* daughter?"

Damn... that blow staggered me. He played the President Obama card. That's like shoving a kryptonite cookie into Superman's mouth—ain't no bouncin' back from that. Round Two ends with me leaning against the ropes, struggling to keep my mouthpiece from falling out.

"I'm a good father. I make sure she has everything she needs and just about anything she wants. Am I as attentive as I should be—probably not. I'll work on that. But, I'm not going to let you, or anyone else, tell me I'm a bad father."

"I never said you were a bad father," Gerald replied calmly. "I said you haven't been giving her enough attention."

I grabbed my fork and stabbed the cube-shaped piece of steak that I'd carved before our tête-à-tête became tense. "I'll take off this Friday and keep her home from school. Maybe take her to lunch and a movie."

"Growing up an only child, my parents gave me everything I ever needed and wanted. I was the first kid in my neighborhood to get a Mongoose bike—one of those real expensive ones—four to five hundred dollars. When I turned sixteen and got a learner's permit, my dad went out and bought me a Toyota Tercel. The rest of my friends were riding the bus to school. After my high school graduation, we returned home and my dream car—a 5.0 Mustang—was in the driveway with a big red bow on it."

"You were a blessed child," I said, wondering where he was going with this story.

"Yes, I was," Gerald mumbled and stared aimlessly at the table. "A few months after I graduated college, my dad had a heart attack. It was bad. I was out of town, so it took me a day or so to get back to be by his side. By the time I arrived, he was coherent enough to hold a conversation, but it was obvious that he wasn't going to last much longer.

"My mother and I rotated spending nights with him at the hospital. The first night was hard for me— watching him doze in and out of consciousness. Tubes coming out of him. Machines beeping and chirping all night. It drove me crazy.

"The second time I was scheduled to go to the hospital and sit with him, I brought a checkerboard. The box it was in was so old that the white parts were pissy-yellow. I opened the box and placed it on the stand where they normally put his food tray. I adjusted his bed so that he could sit up. My dad opened his eyes and asked me in this slurred voice, 'Where'd you get that old checkboard?' I told him it was a gift from him. He said, 'I wouldn't have bought you nothin' that raggedy.'

"I told him the board was raggedy because it was over 15-years-old. He'd bought it for me back when I was around 7- or 8-years-old. During those times when he wasn't traveling on business, which wasn't often, we would sit in our living room and play checkers for hours."

"Did he remember the board after you reminded him?"

"Yes, he remembered. I know he did because the more I talked, the more he smiled and nodded." A tear formed in Gerald's eye. "Out of all the gifts my father ever gave me, that raggedy checkerboard is what I valued the most. It became as important to me as the sun."

"Why?"

"Because when he was in town, that checkerboard was the axis our world orbited around. It was the one thing that gave me his undivided attention."

"Did y'all play checkers that day?"

Gerald nodded and bit his bottom lip. "I made the first move."

"Who won?"

That tear that had been perched on his eyelash fell. Gerald swiped at it and said, "Neither of us. I went to the bathroom after I made my move. When I returned, I noticed he hadn't moved a piece. When I looked at him, I saw him staring up at the ceiling." Gerald looked at me for the first time since he started telling the story. "He was dead."

"Wow." I reached for his hand. "I'm sorry you had to see that."

Gerald pulled his hand back and wiped the trail of tears that streamed down his face.

"I didn't tell you that story to gain sympathy, Ryan. I told you that story to emphasize to you that nothing matters more to children than the time you spend with them. Give her something more than fancy gifts to remember you by."

"I washed my hands, Gee," Suni said. "Can I have some ice cream?"

"Yes, baby. Get it and go in my bedroom. Your daddy's going to come watch television with you."

"Really," Suni said and flashed a thousand-watt smile.

"Yes, *really*," I said and winked. "But it better be good or else I'm going to make you watch something on ESPN."

"No, no, no," Suni said. "I know the perfect movie for us to watch. We're going to watch the new *Aladdin* movie."

Gerald smiled. "You know what else you need to do?" His question was really a demand in disguise.

"What?"

"*You know who*, has been home from the hospital for a while now. It's time you called her so they can talk."

"It's just gon' be more drama. We both know that *you know who* ain't got no damn sense."

"You're probably right, but that doesn't matter. Make the call. It's the right thing to do."

I made it to the third round. Battered and bruised, but in decent enough shape to spend the next two hours enjoying ice cream and *Aladdin* with Suni nestled alongside me.

Chapter 10

MELISSA

I had gained seventeen pounds since being home from my hospital stay. None of my clothes fit so I stayed in sweats and t-shirts to hide my growing hips and waistline. Although, at first, I was eating to prove to my parents and the doctors I was healthy, my taste buds started coming alive and I was eating out of enjoyment. Mama had me in the kitchen helping her cook every meal. She was doing it to keep me busy, I knew that, but I found solace in the sound of the mixer and a boiling pot, nonetheless.

We baked pound cakes, sugar cookies, and lemon meringue pies. We tried new recipes like Beef Wellington and grilled Red Snapper to surprise Daddy with when he came home in the evenings. We even found new recipes for deviled eggs and chicken salad to try out. My mother and I spent hours assisting each other over the island and stove every day, making more food than the three of us could possibly eat so we ended up sharing with neighbors and family that happened to stop by. Everybody left with a care package.

Again, staying busy in the kitchen helped but not enough. I still missed Suni and was eager to get myself together to take Ryan to court. I wasn't afraid to fight him, but my parents were concerned it would send me into an episode. I was glad they were finally seeing Ryan for who he was, even though they still wouldn't admit it to me.

Every day I wondered about Suni missing me, and how sad she must be not being at home. I didn't know how Ryan could sleep at night knowing he was keeping us apart. Yeah, he was selfish and self-centered, but I always thought he had a heart. Even this was a new low for him.

I made regular attempts by phone, text, and email to see Suni, logging it in a notebook so I could have evidence. I would be moving back home this week and returning to work the following Monday. Once I was stable, and he was all comfortable and settled into his role of custodial parent, I was going to gut-punch him with a custody case. Oh yeah, I was walking the line, keeping all my doctor appointments, doing everything they told me, to the point they'd all be ready to go to bat for me to regain custody. I was about to go Claire Huxtable on their asses.

I wasn't dating anyone, I wasn't hanging out—honestly, I wasn't even interested. The only motivation I had was to bring that arrogant fool, to whom I was once married, to his knees. I had the occasional thought of hiring somebody to wipe him out—even daydreamed about it—but the thought would pass me quickly. I didn't really want him to die or for Suni to lose him, I just wanted him to show some compassion towards my situation. After all, he knew I was a good mother at the end of the day.

I had just taken my morning shower and put on a fresh pair of gray sweats, following my morning ritual—at 8:30 a.m. on Mondays, Wednesdays, and Fridays, I opened my notebook and recorded the date and time before sending a cordial text message to Ryan, asking to see Suni. On Tuesdays and Thursdays, I recorded the date and time and called him. Because he never answered my calls, I left a nice voicemail saying the same thing each time. "Hello Ryan, this is Melissa. I would like to see Suni this weekend if she has time in her schedule. Please call me back and let me know. Thank you, goodbye." I had written those words at the top of the page and read them once his voicemail came on. I didn't want him to be able to say I was harassing him. The text message said pretty much the same thing. Both went unanswered or not acknowledgeed.

It was Thursday and I sat at the edge of the bed, holding the phone between my chin and shoulder while the phone rang.

"Hello."

Ryan hadn't taken my calls for so long, I was in stunned silence at the sound of his voice.

"Hello," he said again with less patience.

"Um, Ryan? Oh, hey... This is Melissa."

"I know who it is."

I swallowed, took a deep breath, and spoke up, reading my handwritten words from my notebook. "I would like to see Suni this weekend if—"

"I can drop her off to your parent's home at six-thirty, Friday evening."

A smile crept slowly onto my face. Feeling flustered, I blurted out, "Okay, thank you. I've missed her terribly," my voice cracked.

"Tomorrow at six-thirty and I'll be back to get her on Sunday at the same time. Got it?"

"Got it." I barely got the words out before he disconnected the call.

I tossed the phone on the bed and called him every kind of punk-ass-bitch I could think of. Then I laughed and danced around the room, slipping into my flip-flops, and made my way downstairs. I could see my mother sitting at the breakfast bar holding a coffee mug.

"Mama, Ryan finally answered his phone. I don't know what got into him but he's dropping Suni off tomorrow evening—she's staying until Sunday."

"That's great, sweetheart. I knew he'd come around."

Scrambled eggs, buttery grits, and crispy bacon were keeping warm on the stove, waiting for us to dig in.

"What can we do this weekend when she comes?" I asked my mother for suggestions.

"Well, don't forget you're moving back into your place tomorrow. You did tell Ryan, didn't you?"

"Oh, I totally forgot." I stopped in my tracks, knowing he might have a problem with that.

"You'd better let him know."

"I will..." I was afraid he'd change his mind. That would kill me if he did. I placed plates and glasses on the table.

"Call him back and just tell him you forgot." My mother moved over to the stove and stirred the grits. "If it's an issue, just stay here through the weekend. You can move back home on Monday." She peered over her shoulder. "Just tell him, maybe it'll be okay."

"I will." No, I wouldn't. I didn't have to tell him shit. Suni was my daughter too and wherever I would be, that's where she would be. I was her mother. Before the weekend was up, I'd let him know where to come pick her up—*from home.*

Short of candles on the cake, balloons, and decorations, Mama and Daddy's home would've been mistaken for Suni's birthday party. We had new clothes, shoes, and toys for her, and I even baked her a strawberry cake to celebrate her arrival.

When she and Ryan arrived, I grabbed and kissed her a thousand times, and then put on my fake face for him.

"My baby... Look at you." Once I stopped hugging her, I held Suni by her shoulders, turning her around. It seemed as if she'd grown at least two inches. Her hair was straightened and in two ponytails on either side of her head. "You had her hair pressed?" I peered up at Ryan.

"Actually, she's getting it relaxed now and has an appointment at the salon every other Saturday," he snapped.

"Relaxed? She's too young—you know what, never mind." I wanted to ask him what he knew about a little girl's hair and when chemicals should be introduced but I didn't want my visit to end before it even got started. I turned back to Suni and said, "You look so cute, baby."

I resumed to my fake face, secured Suni inside the house, taking her bags, and turned towards him. "We'll see you Sunday." I moved to close the door, but his hand came up to block me.

"Is your father home? I'd like to speak to him." He moved to step inside but fell back when I stationed my feet.

"Just a minute, I'll get him." I secured the glass door.

While Daddy stepped outside onto the porch, I grabbed Suni again. "Baby, I'm so glad to see you—it's been so long." Tears burned my eyes.

"I missed you too, Mama," she finally said.

"You've gotten so big."

"You have, too," she said to me.

"I know," I answered, trying to laugh but her words stung a little.

"You're fat."

"It's the medication I take—it makes me gain weight like crazy. I know I look a mess." I noticed her blinged-out jeans and Ugg boots. I was glad to see she was being taken care of, but I couldn't help the pangs of jealousy that tugged at my heart. I never thought Ryan couldn't be a good father, he was always that, but I was hoping to spot some deficiencies—something I could put my finger on.

As if she were afraid I wasn't real, Suni gently touched the curls hanging over my shoulders. "You still look pretty," she said to me.

"Hi, baby." Mama stepped into the room, holding her arms open.

"Hi, Nana." Suni went straight to her. "Is all this stuff for me?" she asked, letting go of her grandmother, going straight to the pile of gifts on the fireplace mantel.

"Who else would it be for?" my mother answered.

"I baked your favorite—" I began.

"—Strawberry cake?" Suni peered toward the kitchen.

"But first, let's put your things away." I picked up her fancy new duffle bag and wheeled her matching suitcase, with pink and purple kittens all over it, and headed towards the guest room.

"Can I sleep with you tonight?"

I stopped in my tracks. "I can do better than that. How about we go home and spend the weekend there?"

"We're not staying here at Nana and Grandpa's?"

"We can spend one night here if you want and go home tomorrow."

"My daddy thinks I'm staying here."

"And you will—tonight." When I noticed the look of disapproval on her little face, I lost the little patience I had. "Look, your daddy ain't in charge of me. I'm your mother and I say we're going home tomorrow. Okay?"

"I think I should call him—"

I handed her the duffle bag. "I'll call him myself—here, you take this, and we'll sleep together here, in my room tonight, and then *go home* tomorrow." I wheeled her suitcase to the staircase, and then picked it up to lug it up the stairs. Changing the subject, I said, "Dang girl, what's in here?"

"I brought you a gift. Gee—I mean, Mr. Gerald took me to buy you a gift. He knew how much I missed you, so he asked if I wanted to bring you something." She followed me up the stairs.

"Well, that's sweet." I exhaled loudly, put on a smile, and said, "I'm sure I'll love it."

I was still in denial about Gerald taking my husband from me and wanted to pretend he didn't exist. It was the first time I let myself admit it. But denying his existence was fruitless because the evidence of him was forever present.

Suni plopped onto the floor in my old bedroom and opened her suitcase. She pulled out a large wrapped gift, eager to hand it over. "The bow is smashed a little but Gee—I mean, Mr. Gerald thought it would be best if I put it in the suitcase so Daddy wouldn't see it." She fluffed up the pink bow, and then handed the weighted box to me with both her arms extended.

"Thank you, baby…"

"Open it."

"Why don't we open our gifts together—after dinner? Okay?"

"Please, open it now," she pleaded.

I leaned over, kissed her forehead, and sat on the bed. I pulled apart the wrinkled ribbon and tore open the wrapping paper. Inside the box was a sweatshirt with a picture of Suni and me on the front. There were also bottles of my favorite Sweet Pea shower gel and body lotion.

"I love it—all of it."

"There's something else in the bottom." She peeled back more tissue paper and a silver-framed eight-by-ten picture of her was there.

"Oh, that's why the box was so heavy."

"That's my school picture. I wanted you to have one, too."

"Thank you... It's beautiful."

Damn... I missed picture day.

After dinner and a night full of getting re-acquainted, Suni and I woke up to breakfast, with Nana making her favorite—French toast sprinkled with powdered sugar. We then packed up our stuff, loaded up my BMW, and drove home. Yeah, I could've waited until after Suni was back with Ryan—and maybe should've waited—but I really wanted to settle in before returning to work. My life had been out of sorts for so long, I was desperate for my old routine.

We bounced up the stairs, Suni going straight to her room and I went straight to mine. We unpacked our things, dusted off our dressers, and made a grocery list. I sorted through junk mail and bills. Because I had been on a medical leave, I still received a paycheck, so money was one less thing I had to worry about. Everything was current.

We made a day of it and stopped by the nail salon, getting manis and pedis before heading to the grocery store for food to restock the kitchen. The day was over quickly but we had filled it with fun and laughter. Sunday morning, we met Mama and Daddy at Mount Mariah Baptist Church, the church I'd grown up in, and later, sat around the dining room table, savoring Mama's grilled lamb chops with mint jelly and roasted new potatoes and asparagus. For dessert we finished off the strawberry cake with ice cream.

After sitting around for a while, Suni and I raced home to pack up her things. Ryan said he'd be coming at six-thirty so we had about two hours to go and the fun would end. Realizing this, I felt a rush of emotions but did my best to suppress them. I simply didn't understand why Suni couldn't just come home.

"Make sure you have your stuff together and by the front door when your dad gets here," I told Suni when we stepped into the house, still wearing our Sunday best.

"I will." She trotted up the stairs.

I slipped my cell phone out of my purse and dialed that fool's number.

"Hello," he answered dryly.

"Hey, you need to come pick Suni up at the house."

"Um, yeah—I'll be at your parent's home at six-thirty, like I told you."

"No, we're home. We came home yesterday."

"Melissa, that wasn't the agreement. See, this is why—I'm on my way right now. I knew you couldn't be trusted."

"What's the problem? This is *our* home."

"You don't see what the problem is? The problem is you're a spoiled, crazy bitch thinking rules don't apply to you."

"Who you calling bitch, bitch? You're not the only one that—"

Ryan disconnected the call. I imagined him rushing to his car to race over and start some shit. I'd be ready for his ass, but I called Daddy first.

"Daddy, can you come over? Ryan is on his way and he's mad that we didn't stay there with you guys this weekend."

"I thought you told him—you said you were going to tell him."

"I did—I told him today."

"I'm on my way."

Ryan's main goal was to control every damn thing and to make me appear unstable. He liked working that angle ever since I was diagnosed manic depressive. I wanted to remain calm and reasonable, but I felt it was already too late. He wasn't the type to listen to reason or, for that matter, let me have my way and just let it go.

I paced the kitchen floor in my Red Bottom black stilettos that were growing tighter and tighter with each step I took. My shoes were too tight, and I had squeezed into the only dress that came close to fitting me. I thought about changing clothes but decided maybe Ryan seeing we'd been to church would soften him a bit. Yes, we had spent the morning praising the Lord, ending our perfect weekend of fun and laughter on a holy note. It had all been wonderful, so I hated things were taking a turn, but so be it.

I could hear Suni bringing her bags down, doing just as I'd instructed her.

"Do you have everything?"

"Yes, I think so," she answered from the other room.

"Okay, your dad is on his way now." I peered through the kitchen window, which gave me a view of the street corner I knew Ryan would be coming around.

"When will I be coming back?"

"I'm not sure, but you'll be coming home for good real soon. And I'm sorry this weekend is coming to an end early."

The time on the microwave said four-thirty.

Suni stepped into the kitchen. "It's okay. I forgot I had homework to do anyway."

"You had homework, Suni? I didn't think to even ask you..."

"It's not that much," she insisted. "I can get it done tonight when I get ho—back to Daddy's."

Damn it. That would only give him something else to complain about. It was too late now because just as I'd suspected, Ryan came around the corner on two wheels. I could feel his fire all the way from the street. Suni and I both heard his car door slam from the driveway because we jumped when it did, and seconds later he was laying on the doorbell and banging his fists on the door.

Who the hell does he think he is?

"Is that Daddy?" Suni's face lost its color.

I didn't answer her and just moved to the door. I snatched it open and calmly said, "What the hell is wrong with you banging on my door like you're the police or something?"

"Where's Suni—Suni! Come on, let's go."

"Don't come over here acting a damn fool, Ryan."

"You didn't keep your word so don't expect to see her again for a long time." Ryan stepped in and snatched up Suni's suitcase.

Indignant, I said, "You can't keep my daughter from me." I picked up her duffle bag and held it behind me. "Who the fuck do you think you are?"

"Suni, come on," he yelled over my shoulder, losing his patience.

"She don't have to go no damn where."

Ryan pushed past me, knocking me into the wall. He picked Suni up and headed back towards the door. Still holding the duffle bag, I pulled at Suni's arms, loosening them from his grip. He pushed me again, regaining his hold on Suni. The next thing I knew, my fist landed on the side of his face and he was dragging Suni and me out of the door.

I could hear Suni crying but I wasn't about to let go. I wedged the heel of my shoe at the base of the porch step, giving myself leverage to hold on. Just then, I heard a car door open and close, and saw Gerald racing across the yard. I hadn't seen his face since that horrible day in December.

"Stop it. Y'all, stop it." Gerald placed his hands on Ryan's shoulders. "Suni, you okay? Both of you should be ashamed."

I took notice of my baby, and the anguish on her face gave me pause. Just then, the heel on my shoe gave in, snapping off and forcing me on my knee.

"Are you all right?" Gerald rushed around to help me up, but my adrenaline was at an all-time high. Without realizing what I was doing, I pushed him away.

Daddy's S-Class pulled up to the curb and he jumped out, racing across the yard. "What's going on here?" Daddy helped me to my feet and took the duffle bag from me, with its handles ripped from the fabric, and then handed it to Ryan.

I could feel my knee stinging and blood trickling down my leg. I took off my shoes, standing barefoot on the cold concrete and noticed a rip down the side of my dress. Emotion overtook me, and tears streamed down my face.

Daddy placed a comforting arm around my shoulder and waved Ryan and Gerald on.

Chapter 11

RYAN

I tried... I really did try. As much as I didn't want Suni around Melissa while she was unstable, I listened to Gerald, her father's plea outside of his house, and even allowed myself to be influenced by a scene from that old movie, Kramer vs. Kramer. I listened to every voice except the one I should've listened to—the one inside my head telling me to keep her away.

I do not feel bad about reacting the way I did because she had no right changing the pickup spot. Melissa knows her house has sentimental value. It's only natural that feelings of homesickness would be ignited in Suni once she saw her old bedroom. That's what Melissa's sneaky ass was banking on. She didn't tell me she was going back to her house because she knew I wouldn't have it.

I could hear Suni sniffling in the backseat. I glanced at her in the rearview mirror, but she didn't look up. Her gaze was focused on the floor of the car.

Gerald sat silently. I was familiar with his mannerisms. Every facial expression is made with an intent to either illicit discussion or convey feelings that either time or place prevented from being expressed. Crossed arms coupled with a slow and deliberate head nod conveyed his thoughts—he was riding in the car with a jackass.

"Wipe your face, baby girl," Gerald said and handed her a few pieces of tissue.

"So, you're just gonna sit there and not say anything?" I asked.

"I don't have anything to say now," his words were as lifeless as the tissue he'd just handed Suni, "but trust me, I'll have something to say when we get home. You can take that to the bank."

Great. Now I've gotta deal with one of his lectures, I thought. *Well, he can huff and puff until he's blue in the face, I ain't budging on my position.*

I peeked at the rearview mirror and noticed the dejected look on Suni's beautiful face. "You okay, baby?"

"Leave her alone," Gerald hissed. He rolled his eyes. "You can be so damn tone deaf at times."

"What's that supposed to mean?"

"It means, sometimes you display the emotional intelligence of a rock."

I have no idea what that means, but the shit sounds like a dis, I thought.

Another block passed and he started again. This time he mumbled.

"Smart enough to pass the bar exam, but too thick-headed to know when you're better off being quiet."

My eyes shifted to the rearview mirror to see if Suni would look at me, but she continued to stare out the window. I looked back at Gerald. Between his sulking and Suni's sadness, I wondered if I'd go insane before we made it home.

"You're sitting over there pouting and talking in code. Are you going to get around to saying what's on your mind?"

"Just drive. We'll talk when we get home. I promise you that."

When we walked through the front door, Suni dropped her bags and made a beeline to her bedroom.

"Suni, grab your—"

Gerald cut me off by raising his hand. He grabbed Suni's bag and said, "Like I said... no emotional intelligence."

"Yeah, you keep telling me that, but since you haven't told me what the hell it means, I'm gon' pretend like I didn't hear it." I tossed my car keys on the counter. "I have a headache. I'm goin' to lay down."

Before I could take a third step, a pain shot from between my shoulder blades down to my ass. Gerald had grabbed my car keys and my back was the target.

"What the—"

"Jackass!"

"Why'd you throw the keys at me?"

"You lucky they hit your back. I was aiming for your head."

"What the fuck's wrong with you?"

Gerald marched up to me and punched me in the chest.

"You are what the *fuck* is wrong with me!"

I'd been punched in the face by Melissa and now Gerald was beating on me. Melissa's blow bruised my flesh; whereas, Gerald's blow bruised my flesh, ego, and feelings. I took a step backward while I delivered my message.

"Make that the last time you hit me."

I could feel my desire to fight growing more belligerent—tussling and pleading to be unleashed like the Hulk just under the surface of David Banner's skin.

"Or what?" Gerald asked flippantly. "You gon' run up on me the way you did that child's mother."

97

"I was just trying to get Suni."

"No, what you did was overreact the way you always do when it comes to Melissa. It's like you lose your damn mind."

"How am I overreacting? We had an agreement—I'd let Suni stay with her for the weekend. They were supposed to stay at her parent's house. She changed the plan without telling me. If the shoe was on the other foot, and I did some shit like that, the courts would be trying to ban me from seeing my child."

"Stop exaggerating. This isn't a courtroom and there's no jury or judge here to impress."

"I'm not exaggerating. If Melissa had custody of Suni, and I changed the plan without telling her, all she'd have to do is mention that shit to a judge and that's all the excuse he'd need to keep me from my child. When it comes to custody, the courts are biased as hell. They treat daddies like fucking wallets. Like we're incompetent and incapable of being the better parent. You got a lot of fucked up mothers out there too, and Melissa's crazy ass is one of 'em."

Gerald folded his arms and shook his head in that slow "oscillating fan" type of motion. The pity in his eyes made me angrier.

"If you think I overreacted, then too fucking bad. I'm reacting the same way her—and every other manipulative-ass woman out there—has reacted for decades. Every time she violates, I'm gon' say something. I'm documenting every time she's late dropping her off. Every time she does something that's contrary to what we agreed on. Hell, if that bitch farts around my child, I'm documenting that too."

"That's just petty," Gerald said.

"You call it petty, I call it beating her ass to the punch." As if the word "punch" sent my nerve endings into a panic, a flash of pain seized the side of my face. I touched the spot, and I could feel the welt that formed on my cheekbone. "And I'm gon' take a picture of my face so the judge can see that she punched me—again."

Gerald threw up his hands and pivoted in the direction of Suni's bedroom. He took a few steps and stopped. Like a soldier, he did an about-face and walked toward me. "You know, I've been by your side during all of this. I supported your efforts to get Suni because I honestly felt it was best for her. Now, I'm starting to wonder if you are a part of the problem and not the solution."

Yes, I'm gay, but I'm still a man with pride. And no man—not even a gay man—wants to be beat up by a woman.

Dating back to my elementary school days, I was trained to never hit a girl. It was a lesson taught to me—better yet, beat into me—back when I punched the hell out of Jemice Connors and nearly choked the shit out of Trina Dupree, two girls in my fourth-grade class who bullied me incessantly.

Every day in class, Jemice would pass my desk and smack the back of my head. Trina, who sat behind me, would pinch the back of my arm—that fleshy part under the biceps that hurts like hell when squeezed.

One day during recess, I told our chain-smoking teacher, Ms. Hobbs, about their harassment. Ms. Hobbs, who often hid in a corner of the playground out of the sight of any co-worker who might snitch while she stole a few puffs off a cigarette, blew a cloud of smoke in my direction and said, "Boy, those little girls are just sweet on you. They mess with you because they like you. You're complaining now, but in ten years, you're gon' be chasin' them."

She dismissed me with a wave of her cigarette clutching hand. I returned to the jungle gym where Hurricanes Jemice and Trina waited and tried to stay away from them. I could feel their mischievous stares. When I moved to one side of the jungle gym, they followed. When I moved to the hot ass metal sliding board, they followed. They trailed me like two lionesses waiting for the right moment to pounce on a gazelle. When there was no place left for me to hide, I decided to confront them. But, when I spun to face them, only Jemice was standing there.

"Why y'all keep followin' me?"

"Ain't nobody followin' you. You ugly—we wouldn't follow you anyway."

"Y'all been followin' me. If y'all keep followin' me—"

"What you gon' do?"

Jemice moved closer. She placed her hand on her boney hip. Beads of sweat lined the top of her forehead. Her chocolate skin glistened, but the moisture stopped at her hair line, fearful to venture into that dirty forest she called hair.

I tried to maintain eye contact with her, but my eyes kept shifting to the bushel of hair she pulled back. Her hair was too short to make a ponytail, so a thick green rubber band had the unfortunate task of keeping that stub of a plait—that looked like a plant that managed to grow out of a used Brillo Pad—in place.

"I'm gon' punch you if you keep followin' me."

Jemice moved closer. She was so close I could see the sleep still caked in the corner of her eyes. She pointed her finger, with its peeling red polish, at the tip of my nose. "I'd like to see you try it."

I was about to fire off a comeback that was going to include her nappy hair, bad breath, unwashed face, and chipped fingernail polish, but a breeze swooped up from my ankles and chilled my tiny balls.

Every child on that playground stopped what they were doing and looked at me. A wave of laughter, the likes of which is only heard at the Apollo Theatre in New York when a singer gets ushered off stage by the Sandman, swirled. I wasn't sure what happened until I realized that every child out there was pointing at me. And they weren't pointing at my face, they were pointing at my crotch.

I'd been outmaneuvered. Jemice and Trina had set me up. While Jemice kept me talking, Trina flanked me and snuck up from my rear. She yanked down my shorts and exposed the Star Wars underwear I'd begged my mother to buy.

That was it. They'd pushed me too far.

Trina was bent over laughing. I pulled up my shorts and put her in a headlock that would have put a professional wrestler to shame. I clamped down on her neck like a vice grip and squeezed until she screamed.

Jemice charged and pummeled me with a barrage of blows, but I refused to let go. I was intent on wringing Trina's scrawny neck until she begged me to stop.

I managed to fire off a stiff jab at Jemice and connected with her nose. Blood sprayed her shirt and mine. The blood was the only thing that stopped the other children from laughing, and the only thing that made me release Trina.

Ms. Hobbs managed to put down her cigarette long enough to wobble her fat ass over and do her job. At five-two and weighing in at around three hundred pounds, it took her awhile to get to us, but by the time she did, I knew I was in trouble. Jemice bled like a stuck pig and Trina had the snot-nose ugly face cry because her bifocal glasses were destroyed while I had her in a headlock.

Ms. Hobbs grabbed my ear and twisted until I was damn near on my knees pleading. She led me straight to the principal's office.

Mr. Brumfield, a mountain of a man, believed in corporal punishment. Because he stood more than six-feet tall, his huge belly made him look like a walking bowling pin. Inside of his office, he kept a huge paddle. There was a leather strap at the end—what he slipped his hand in to make sure he didn't drop it when he swung—and it hung on a rusty nail. Etched on the paddle was the phrase: *The Peacekeeper*.

If I could press charges against him right now for the ass-whooping he gave me that day, I would. To make matters worse, when I got home, my dad opened a can of whip-ass on me that I'll never forget. *'Don't. Hit. Girls'*, was his chant while he *hit me* for twenty consecutive minutes. I made a promise to my dad that I'd never raise my hands to a girl again.

As I stared at my puffy eye in my bathroom mirror, I wondered if it was time to break that promise. This was the second time since our divorce that Melissa hit me and got away with it. If I struck back, no juror in his or her right mind would be able to go against me. Even a blind person could see it was self-defense.

I placed a cold towel on my eye and thought about the new leverage I had. Yes, my face stung like hell, but this pain would be my gain. I grabbed my cellphone and I took a dozen pictures from every angle. I then dialed my lawyers' number and texted each photo with the caption:

> Me: This happened
> to me 30 minutes
> ago when I went to
> pick up Suni.

Janice texted me back within seconds.

> Janice: Are you okay?

Me: Yes. My ego is
as bruised as my
face, but I'll
survive.
Janice: Were the
police involved?

I immediately knew where she was going with that question.

Me: No. Should I
call them?
Janice: Did you hit
her?
Me: No. Wanted to
but didn't. I
grabbed Suni and
got out of there.
Janice: Good. File a
police report
TODAY! We got her
ass.

My pit bull in a skirt was ready for war. I called the police just like Janice instructed and waited patiently for the familiar heavy-handed law enforcement knock at my front door.

While waiting for the police to arrive, several things marched across my mind: Did my daughter hate me? Was Gerald turned off by my actions? Was I, in fact, wrong for exercising my rights as a father?

As much as I wanted to appear confident in my position and not show any signs of wavering, the desire to know what Suni and Gerald felt gave me pause. The thought nagged like an itch in the center of your back that's hard to reach. I tried my hardest to avoid going upstairs, but I couldn't. Before I knew it, I was tiptoeing up the stairs and had my ear pressed to Suni's bedroom door.

"C'mon, baby girl, I need you to take your face out of the pillow and talk to me," Gerald said. "I can't help you if you won't talk to me."

I heard Suni whimpering. The bed sheets rustled and then she asked, "Why does Daddy hate Mommy?"

"He doesn't hate her. They just argue sometimes."

"He does hate her. That's why he doesn't want me around her. Mommy told me that Daddy doesn't want me to live with her anymore. She said he's trying to take me away."

"That's not true, Suni. Both of your parents love you. Sometimes adults have arguments. Unfortunately, you saw something today that a child should never have to see. But I promise you, things will get better. I promise you, I'm not going to let anything like this happen again. You're going to be safe here."

"I don't want to stay here anymore. I want to go back to my mom."

Her words scurried up my arms like a centipede and made the hairs stand up. This wasn't the stammering of a frantic child. She spoke with clarity and conviction.

"Are you hungry?" Gerald asked, trying to change the subject.

Suni didn't answer.

"Why don't you lay down and get some rest. I'll come up in about an hour with some food. Is pizza okay?"

"Yes."

I could hear Gerald stand up. I pivoted and was halfway down the steps when Suni's bedroom door opened. I froze like a roach when the lights come on. Gerald closed the door and elbowed me in the side as he moved past and headed down the stairs.

"Did you hear everything?" he asked rhetorically. "Probably had your ear pressed against the door."

I didn't respond; sometimes you must accept that you've been busted and move on. Instead, I went to the front door and waited with it partially open.

"What's out there?"

"I'm waiting for the police," I replied and continued to look outside.

"What?"

"You heard me; the police are on their way," I responded, without glancing back.

"Why?"

"Because Janice told me to call them. I need to have these bruises and details about her attack documented."

Gerald glared. "Talk to them outside," he said and shoved me.

"Why?"

"Because I said so, goddammit! That child is traumatized. The last thing she needs to see are police in here questioning you. I do not want them in this house."

"Fine."

Gerald stood as stiff as the spindles on the staircase. We'd had our share of arguments—dirty dishes left on the kitchen counter; toothpaste traces left in the bathroom sink; even moments of being too friendly to strangers; but his eyes held a sentiment that was foreign to me—at least coming from him. For the first time in our relationship, Gerald looked at me with disgust.

"You know, you may win this battle, but you're gonna lose the war."

"What are you trying to say?"

"I'm sayin', you are gonna fuck around and make your daughter resent you."

"No, she won't. I'm protecting her."

"Really? You think she feels like she needs to be protected from her mother?"

"Yes, I do. I'm her father. It's my job to make these kinds of decisions on her behalf. She's too young to know what she needs or feels. Isn't that the kind of stuff women say every time they want to do what they feel is best for a child?"

Gerald moved close enough to convey his thought with a whisper. "While you're down here selling Melissa out to the cops, you need to remember what you heard while you were eavesdropping at Suni's door. She's ready to go back home to her mother."

Gerald paused when we heard the doors of the police car close.

"They're here," I said.

Gerald looked me up and down the way foes do moments before a fight.

"While you're out there whining to the police, let them know that your daughter is terrified of you."

Chapter 12

MELISSA

I had been back to work for a couple of days, feeling unwelcome and totally out of place. I was the last of the employed graphic designers hired for the Kroger Company, the rest were contract workers, and I knew that was the only reason they kept me. I had been there for twelve years. They had to. Well, *and* I was highly skilled. I was sure at first that they missed me being there to handle my forever-heavy load, but clearly, they'd found a way to keep things moving without me, ultimately rendering me expendable. But because of the law, they kept me, treating me with kid gloves, pretending they were happy to have me back.

Yes, some co-workers were genuinely glad to see that I was well, but there were others that didn't bat an eye when I took a seat behind my dusty desk, which had been moved to the back in a lonely corner.

I was three days in, and it took that long to get up to speed on the new projects and work load I was facing, all while popping Ibuprofen to ward off the painful bruises and muscle aches from Sunday's tussle with Ryan. I did my best not to focus on that situation so I could be mentally present for work, but the scene constantly replayed in my mind.

It was Wednesday and I stopped by Pei Wei on the way home, picking up a bowl of noodles topped with chicken and shrimp. The plan was to sit in front of the TV, eat my food, check in with Mama and Daddy—maybe even return old messages from when I was out of pocket, and then go to bed. But, the best laid plans of mice and men...

I pulled into the garage, rushed through the door, and tossed my purse and food on the kitchen table before racing to the powder room. Coming home, for some reason, was a trigger to have to urgently pee. It had been that way since I was a kid. Step through the door, pee, wash my hands. It was a habit I thought little of.

I kicked off my boots and was about to settle into my, what I still imagined was warm, dinner when there was a knock at the door, followed by the doorbell. I found the order of that to be odd, so I discretely peeked out the dining room window.

A Dallas police squad car was parked at the curb and two officers were on my porch. *What the fuck?*

I paced for a second and grabbed my cell phone from my purse.

"Daddy—" I uttered before he could even say hello. "The police are at my door."

The doorbell rang again, which I imagined he heard.

"The police?" He took a beat and said, "Go ahead and answer it, but don't hang up. I want to hear. I'm headed that way."

I slipped the phone in a pocket of the sweater I was wearing and went to the door. I took in a deep breath and unlocked it, pulled it open, and turned on the light in the foyer.

"Yes, can I help you?"

For years, Ryan and I argued over getting a storm door. I wanted one and he didn't. I wanted to be able to open the interior door during spring and fall afternoons so I could see out and into the neighborhood. He thought it was ghetto, saying that most of the homes in the area didn't have storm doors, reminding me that we didn't live in the country or the 'hood. As always, he got his way. I promised myself once he was out, I would get that storm door but had never gotten around to it. How I desperately wished I had another line of defense between the officers and me. In the end, would it matter? No. But I felt so exposed standing there within arm's reach of the two men in front of me that I had no way of knowing if they were friend or foe.

"I'm Officer Caprio and this is Officer Tact. Are you Melissa Gray?" The smaller man, who stood in front, spoke up first.

I could hear my heart thumping like a bass guitar, having a full-fledge concert inside my chest. Images of Justine Damond, Rekia Boyd, Robin Pearson, and Sandra Bland—all women who ended up dead after interacting with the police—blinded my vision. I couldn't hear. I couldn't see. I couldn't think.

"Ma'am, are you Melissa Gray?" he repeated and took a step forward.

I wasn't going to lie about who I was, but I wanted to know why they were there. I also wanted to ask Daddy what I should do.

"What is this about?" I reached for the phone in my pocket.

"Ma'am, please don't place your hands in your pocket." He took another step forward and the taller officer took one step back, surveying the front of the house. "Identify yourself, please."

"Oh—it's just my phone—"

"Leave it in your pocket." His hand then rested on his gun.

"Yes—yes, I'm Melissa. What's this about?" The cold breeze rushing in did nothing to stop the sweat running down my back.

"Melissa, we have a warrant for your arrest for assault. Can you step outside?"

"Assault?" By this time, I had my phone in my hand and the officer had me by the wrist before I could put it up to my ear. "Assaulting who?"

"Please, let go of the phone. You're under arrest for assaulting Ry..."

"No—no, let me call—"

"I can give you a moment to put some shoes on, but you'll get a chance to make a phone call after you're booked," he said, holding my phone.

I had no way of knowing if Daddy was still on an active call, but I was praying he was.

I couldn't believe it. *Ryan is really trying to take me down*, was all I could think while an officer of the law stood before me holding handcuffs, waiting on me to put my boots back on and grab my keys. I moved as slowly as I could, trying to give Daddy time to arrive but it wasn't until the squad car turned the corner, with me restrained in the back seat, did I see the headlights of Daddy's S-Class coming up the street.

This was a new low for everybody involved. But for me, something had changed. I was now a woman with a police record. I vacillated between feeling sorry for myself and plotting a payback on that motherfucker. I honestly couldn't believe he'd taken it this far. I was the mother of his only child and he wanted me in jail. I was a woman he used to love—didn't that count for something?

It was 7:30 a.m. and I was sitting in the passenger seat next to Daddy. He'd bailed me out just in time to get home, shower, and be at work on time. There was no way I could miss any more days.

"Are you all right, baby?"

"No, I'm not all right." I shifted in my seat, unable to keep still. "Maybe now you'll see what I've been saying about Ryan." I envisioned holding-cell bacteria and jail residue all over me.

"He didn't have to do that—press charges. He had a little scratch on his face, but you looked worse than he did—dress all torn up—knee bleeding." Daddy was finally angry. "You should've called the police on him first." His breathing was heavy and labored. "You have to appear in court next Monday—can you take off?"

"I'll tell them I have a doctor appointment—they won't question that."

"I really wish you two would stop all this fighting. If for no one else, for Suni. All this ain't good for her—she doesn't deserve it."

The car pulled into my driveway and I exhaled a little, relieved to be home. I was exhausted but was going to have to pull it together and start my day.

"I'm not trying to fight with him—"

"—You need to stop provoking him," my father interrupted. "You should've done like I told you and let him know where you were going to be."

I had my hand on the door handle, ready to get out. I knew Daddy didn't totally blame me, but I couldn't stand that he wouldn't see things from my perspective. "You know he would've taken her if I said we were going home—you know he would've. The fight just would've happened sooner."

"Well, maybe. But you still have to do the right thing, no matter what. That's all I'm saying." He put the car in park. "If a judge sees you doing all the right things, that can only help you."

"I know," I conceded, anxious to get out of the car. "I'll call you later. Thanks, Daddy." I swung open the car door. "I'll pay you back the twenty-five hundred dollars—I promise."

Daddy just grunted. I imagined him, in his head, tacking that amount onto the many thousands I already owed him—money he knew he'd never see again.

"You and Ryan just get it together," he said between gritted teeth as I was closing the car door.

With my door keys in one hand and my cellphone in the other, I heavily made my way up to the house. I didn't turn back and wave but heard his car shift into gear as I stepped across the threshold.

As soon as I secured the lock, I stripped off my clothes, stepped into the shower with the water as hot as I could stand it, washing myself from head to toe. I dried off, towel dried my hair, massaged curling cream into it, and combed out the tangles. I quickly dressed and made my way downstairs to throw out last night's uneaten dinner that still sat on the kitchen table. I placed one of Suni's Pop-Tarts in the toaster and ate it on the way to work, chasing it down with that morning's dose of drugs to ward off my demons. It was going to be a long day.

On Friday, I found myself back in Norvelle Kates's office. Although we had spoken on the phone a few times, several months had passed since I'd been there. I was nervous about what we faced, but I was anxious to get things going again.

"So, how are you doing, Melissa?" Norvelle sat behind his huge desk, leaning back in his chair with his clasped hands under his chin. He wore a fitted royal blue suit, crisp white shirt, a speckled tie with a Windsor knot.

"I'm good, thanks." I was seated in front of him with my one leg crossed over the other, purse resting in my lap, doing my best to appear clear and calm.

"You look well," he said with some surprise in his voice, nodding as if he were sizing me up. "That's good to see."

"Yeah, for me too."

"Before we get into why you're here, I want you to know that we're still moving forward with the fight for full-custody. However, I wanted to propose to you that we wait until you've been back at work for six months to show stability. What do you think?"

"No, I don't want to wait. I want my daughter to come home now. She's been gone too long already."

"Showing stability will only help the judge rule in our favor, that's all."

"No, the longer she's with him and he has control, the harder it will be to get her back. No."

"Do me a favor and take a week to think on it. Six months isn't as long as it sounds." He leaned forward and picked up a piece of paper on his desk. "I have your summons to appear in court on Monday and I'll be there with you. Ryan will be there too, bringing assault charges against you. The judge will then decide whether or not to prosecute." Without any change in his expression, Norvelle said, "Tell me what happened."

I shifted in the chair and cleared my throat. "I had been trying for months to see Suni, with Ryan totally ignoring me. Finally, he agreed to let her come for a weekend visit to my parents while I was staying with them—you know—from my stint in the hospital. Anyway, he agreed to let her come and I forgot to tell him that I had already been planning to go home that weekend. Once I remembered, I was afraid he would change his mind if I told him. So, I waited until it was time for him to come pick her up to let him know we were home. When he cussed me out and hung up on me, I knew it was gonna be trouble. He sped over to my house, stormed up to the door, and rushed in. We had a tug-o-war with Suni, and he dragged me out of the house, while I hung on to her."

"Did you hit him?"

"Yeah, I clocked his ass."

"Did he hit you?"

"Well—we assaulted each other." I tried remembering if Ryan ever hit me that day. I couldn't think of any occasion when he had; but he had done so much foul shit, I felt like he suffered no consequences for, I just didn't want to let him off the hook. "I had injuries—broke the heel off my shoe—ripped my dress—bloody knee."

"Did he put his hands on you?" he repeated.

"We put hands on each other."

Norvelle tapped a lone finger on his desk while making eye contact with me. "Okay—okay..."

Monday morning, we stood in front of Judge Christine White, a tiny Caucasian woman in her fifties, sporting a jet-black page boy. I was on one side of the courtroom with Norvelle, and Ryan was on the other side with his team of golden boys with one sharp-looking sister leading the pack. Mama and Daddy were seated in the front row, watching on, and one row behind them, so was the man that stole my husband.

Everything happened so quickly I could hardly keep up. Ryan, looking like he was fresh off the cover of *GQ* magazine, smug expression and all, presented ten pages of pictures from multiple angles of his bruised face from the sucker punch I'd delivered.

"Your Honor, I was simply picking up my daughter when Ms. Gray attacked me just like she has on several occasions. This was the first time I decided to report it. I was tired of her abuse. She has slapped me, punched me, kicked me..."

I couldn't believe the embellishments coming from his mouth—but then again, I could.

"Mr. Gray, before you go on, I only want to hear about the day in question," the judge spoke up and stopped his lies. "That's all we're here for."

"We just wanted you to have some background, Your Honor," his attorney spoke up.

"Ms. Mower, I don't need background at this time—just the facts of that day."

"I understand, Your Honor."

"Continue," Judge White instructed Ryan.

"When I arrived, I rang the doorbell and she let me in. Once I was in, she started her verbal assault as usual, cursing me out in front of our daughter, calling me out of my name. All I wanted to do was get Suni and leave. When I picked up my daughter and her suitcase, that's when Ms. Gray landed the punch to my face and tried taking her from me—refusing to let me leave with her. I struggled to get out the door and once we ended up on the porch, my husband got out the car to intervene and that's when she took a swing at him too. When my former father-in-law arrived moments later, he was able to calm her down and my husband and I took my daughter and left to avoid any further abuse from Ms. Gray. Your Honor, I never know when she's on or off her medication, so I do my best to avoid her."

That last part he said was to twist the knife—I knew that. I didn't even have to turn my head to see that Ryan was feeling pretty satisfied with himself from the testimony of lies he'd given. I was burning hot and sensed the judge was taking all that bullshit in. I glanced back at Daddy and he slowly shook his head, trying to calm me down. Just then, I felt Norvelle's hand cover my own.

"It's cool, don't worry."

"Mr. Kates, how does your client respond to these allegations?"

Norvelle stood and leaned on the table in front of us. "Self-defense, Your Honor. When you're ready, we'd like to present our own evidence."

"When I'm ready? What do you think we're here for, Mr. Kates? Don't waste my time—get on with it."

"I have no intention to waste your time." He shifted and stood straight. "The story of Mr. Gray *calmly* coming to pick up his daughter is simply not true, and I'd like to present evidence of that." He held up his iPad. "We have video from two different neighbors' surveillance cameras showing just how calmly Mr. Gray arrived that afternoon, before he stormed through the doors and initiated what became mutual combat. Your Honor, he provoked the whole incident that day."

The bailiff handed over the iPad to the judge and they all waited in silence as she viewed the recording.

When Norvelle told me to ask my neighbors if they had cameras, I thought he was joking. It seemed like a waste of time and I really didn't want them in my business until the new neighbors across the street provided me with everything I needed. I'd viewed the tape so many times, I knew exactly what the judge was taking in. The first neighbor's video started from one angle of Ryan's BMW racing around the corner, hitting the curb before stopping in front of my driveway with one tire up in the grass. The tape then transitions to another neighbor's footage from a different angle of him swinging his car door open, racing up the yard, pounding on my door, and pushing his way in. Nothing like he'd described just moments before.

Judge White slowly peered up from the screen, gave a blank stare towards Ryan and his team, and then handed the iPad to the bailiff. "Let them see this."

Norvelle and I gave each other a smirk.

Once the iPad was handed back to Judge White, she spoke up. "You know, I've been ruling on these kinds of cases for over twenty years and the one thing I've learned, if nothing else, is that no one wins. And the biggest losers of all are the children involved." She took turns giving Ryan and me both the stink eye. "You two appear to be well-educated, normal people—which most litigants in front of me do. I know you both love your daughter—that's not a question. The problem is, you don't love her more than you hate each other.

"It is clear to me that Mr. Gray has watered down his part of that day's interaction—and I'm sure Ms. Gray will do the same, claiming he hit her first, etcetera. Mr. Gray, once you pushed your way into what I assume used to be your home, it is your word against hers on what happened next. Now, to the both of you, did either of you, when watching this video, notice the trauma on your daughter's face or were you too busy looking at the other person, ready to build your case against her or him?" She pointed at Ryan and then at me. "I can prosecute you both for assault, but what will that get us? More loss for your daughter—that's all." She took in a labored breath and let it out slowly. "What I would like to propose to you two fine-looking people..." She looked at papers in front of her. "... Suni's parents, is to drop all of the charges with the promise of the two of you loving your daughter more than your desire to bring each other down."

Tears burned my eyes. I never meant for things to go this far. I couldn't remember Suni in that video. In that moment, I remembered her crying that day, but I had blocked it out. Shame silently rushed over me like cancerous radiation, killing every cell in my body. I wanted to die—and I wanted to live, if for no other reason than having a chance to get it right.

"I understand that there is also a custody case going on, too. Do you really want to take the other parent away from Suni? Is that your goal?" After a pregnant pause, Judge White spoke clearly, "Where is your decency? If you truly love your daughter, it's not that difficult to work together for the good of the person you love most in common. Am I right?"

"Yes, Your Honor," I heard Ryan say.

"Yes," I added. "Yes, ma'am."

"Stop focusing on why you split up—let that go. Move on with your respective lives. When dealing with the ex-spouse, do everything with your daughter's best interest in mind. And with that being said, can you both agree to stop this nonsense and move forward with an arrangement that works for both of you? Because if I see you again over these same allegations or something similar, you're both going to jail. What do you say?"

"Yes, Your Honor," Ryan spoke up first again.

Just as she turned to me, I said, "Yes, Your Honor. I agree."

"Charges have been dropped and case dismissed." The gavel came down loudly as Judge White stood to leave the courtroom.

I felt good. I felt hopeful. I was encouraged that life was returning to normal. If only working with Ryan could be that simple. I'll be damned if he didn't go right back to controlling every damn thing, putting my patience to the test—pushing me to my limits. *I'll just be damned.*

Chapter 13

RYAN

On the surface, Judge White's ruling may have appeared fair and unbiased, but I didn't see it that way. As far as I was concerned, she was another female judge giving a woman a break in family court.

Now, I may be a lot of things, but stupid ain't one. So, when Judge White instructed Melissa and me to *play nice*, I looked right at her and said, *Yes*. I even offered a subservient bow—the kind southern black folk mastered during the Jim Crow Era.

There was an eerie silence on the home front those next couple of days after our court appearance. By mid-week, Gerald and I felt we needed to get out of the house, so we decided to go to Bone Fish Grill to have a nice, quiet dinner. The food wasn't great, but the restaurant's ambiance was calming; the atmosphere I needed to take the edge off... along with a few stiff Kettle One martinis.

"You've been quiet for the past two days," Gerald said. He used a toothpick to spear the olive floating in his drink and popped it into his mouth. "I know you are under a lot of stress, so I've been trying to give you space. Even though I haven't always agreed with the way you've handled things, I want you to know that I'm still here for you."

I nodded and sipped my drink.

Gerald sighed. "Baby, don't shut me out. I'm not your enemy. I need you to open up and talk. Tell me how you're feeling."

"You wanna know how I'm feeling?"

"Yes, I do. I'm your husband. We should be able to agree to disagree."

"You really wanna know how I feel right now?"

"Yes, I do."

I ate the olive in my martini and guzzled the drink.

"Ooookay," Gerald said. "I have a feeling that I'm going to regret asking you to open up."

I shrugged. "You shouldn't. Didn't you just say we can agree to disagree?"

"Yes, I did."

I looked around for our waiter. When I spotted him, I pointed to my glass to signal I needed another drink. I stared at Gerald. Behind his blank gaze I could see eyes that were fearful I was about to combust. He had a reason to be concerned.

"I've been thinking about us."

"You and me?" Gerald asked, his words laced with surprise.

"Yes... us."

"And what are your thoughts regarding us?"

"I think I know why we've been off balance lately."

"And why is that?"

"Do you know the difference between sympathy and empathy?"

Gerald stared at me for a moment and then lifted his drink to his lips. Before he took a sip, he said, "I assumed they were synonymous, but I have a feeling you're going to tell me different."

"It's easy to have sympathy for the problems a person is going through," I said. "Especially, if you are a caring person." I pointed at Gerald. "You have a huge heart. Sympathy is your default. Unfortunately, you don't seem to understand that sympathy is a spectator sport."

"Here is your martini, sir," said the waiter and placed the drink on the table "May I get you anything else?"

"I'll take another," Gerald said.

"Another martini coming up," the waiter said and walked away.

I savored my drink and then continued. "Where was I?"

"You were breaking down the difference between sympathy and empathy."

"Oh, yeah... like I said, sympathy is a spectator sport."

"I caught that," Gerald said. "It doesn't require participation; you just observe the other person's pain."

"Exactly. It's kind of like watching a woman deal with labor pains. You can only sympathize with her because it's not a pain you've ever experienced. In order to be able to empathize with her, you need to have experienced labor pains in your life." I pointed the plastic toothpick that had been in my glass at him. "And that's where we've been having our problems. You love me, so naturally you have sympathy for what I'm going through. But you've never been a parent. Well, you're a stepparent now, but I'm talking about being the biological parent of a child. Which means, you've never had to deal with the bullshit that comes with co-parenting with a selfish baby-mama. Therefore—"

"Since I don't have that experience, I can only have sympathy for what you're going through, but I can't empathize with you."

"Ding, ding, ding," I said sarcastically. "Someone give this man a prize."

"Touché. I can't argue that point, counselor. But, I don't have to be able to empathize with you to see that you're taking things too far."

"Why? Because I'm fighting for my daughter."

Gerald lifted his drink and said in a hushed tone before taking a sip, "Lower your voice, Ryan."

"My bad," I said and disposed of my martini with one gulp. "I just get frustrated."

"About what, exactly?"

"The entitled way women act when it comes to raising kids. As if God stated somewhere in the Bible that women were gifted with a parenting gene that's superior to what a man has."

"You're entitled to your feelings. I don't know this to be true, but I'm guessing some women feel like that because of the bond they form with the baby while it's in their body for nine months. The joy and the pain that comes with that experience creates a special connection."

"Special connection my ass!" I blurted out.

From my peripheral, I could see the couple at a nearby table look our way. Gerald's demeanor didn't change. In his typically calm demeanor, he sipped his drink and then leaned back in his chair. Not a word was uttered, but his sentiment was conveyed loud and clear via his piercing stare.

"I'm sorry, baby."

"Continue," Gerald said.

"I just get so frustrated with that canned response. Carrying a child for nine months doesn't make a woman a better parent. God designed her body to be the incubator. Whatever pain that comes with that job, they should take that shit up with God; men ain't got nothing to do with that. What I do know is that if it weren't for the man's sperm, a woman wouldn't have a baby to carry. So, as far as I'm concerned, a man has just as much claim to be the primary caregiver as a woman."

"I don't think the judge said that."

"She didn't have to say it. Her actions did the talking."

"How so?"

A part of me wanted to lean across that table and shake the hell out of Gerald. I felt the situation was as clear as day and shouldn't have to be explained. Then I remembered—he could only *sympathize* with me, not *empathize*.

"Babe, if Melissa had presented the same pictures that showed proof of physical abuse, not only would the judge have ruled in her favor, I would have been arrested for assault and taken out of that courtroom in handcuffs. That court proceeding was just another example of how biased the system is."

"I can't argue with that. I must admit, I was surprised those pictures didn't have a greater impact."

"You damn right, they should've. The courts bend over backwards to support women. All men are good for is our bank accounts; keep the child support checks coming and shut up. The minute the child becomes too much for them to handle, the first thing they do is say, 'I'm gon' call your daddy.' All that does is set up a barrier between the father and the child. We can be the enforcers, but we ain't good enough to be the primary caregivers."

I got the waiter's attention and pointed at my glass again.

"That's your last one," Gerald said.

"I'm a grown man."

Gerald squinted and strummed his fingers on the table.

"Fine," I grunted. "Anyway, that's why I'm fighting so hard to keep custody of Suni. I'll be damned if I allow myself to be relegated to being the "bad guy" when there are disciplinary issues, so she can be the cool parent when the waters are calm. I intend to change the paradigm—Suni is going to live in a house with two loving fathers that show her that the men in her life are more than ATM machines."

Gerald sighed and finished his drink.

"The way I see it, the judge made it very clear that she doesn't want to see the two of you back in her court with that foolishness. So, I need you to start thinking of ways to be a part of the solution to this mess and not a part of the problem."

"I'm going to keep doing things the way I always have—by the book."

"Good. We may not like the judge's ruling, but it beats being in her doghouse."

The stress of my life introduced a new challenge—insomnia. For most of my adult life, I bragged about my ability to carve out seven to nine hours of sleep every night. Since Judge White's tongue lashing and with the constant fear of losing custody of my child looming over me like bruised rain clouds ready to burst, I was lucky to corral three to five hours of sleep a day.

Gerald and I showered after we returned from dinner that evening. Within minutes, he was in a coma-like sleep. I, on the other hand, couldn't have found sleep if I had a flashlight and it was the size of a Yeti.

As had become my habit, I took a Benadryl pill, poured myself a glass of Apple Brandy, and grabbed a book to read until I dozed off. I don't know if my literary selection was subconscious, but the book I grabbed when I blindly reached for my shelf was *The Art of War* by Sun Tzu. Apropos—maybe. Dangerous—certainly.

I'd read *The Art of War* several times, but I always enjoyed going back to it because I'd see something I missed during previous readings. On this sleep deprived evening, my go-to manuscript didn't let me down. My eyes rested on this quote from the book:

"For to win one hundred victories in one hundred battles is not the acme of skill. To subdue the enemy without fighting is the acme of skill. Hence to fight and conquer in all your battles is not supreme excellence; supreme excellence consists in breaking the enemy's resistance without fighting."

Amid the darkness that engulfed me at that moment, the light bulb inside of my head flickered and then shined bright enough to illuminate the entire house.

"That's it," I muttered. "I've been going about this all wrong. I've been so busy challenging Melissa, that I'm not using the one thing I have over her—my brain. Instead of outthinking her, I've dumbed down my tactics to match hers. That's why we're at a stalemate."

I read some more and stumbled on another thought-provoking quote:

"Let your plans be dark and impenetrable as night, and when you move, fall like a thunderbolt."

That quote brought life to my weary eyes. I knew it was meant to be applied to two people—Melissa and Gerald.

I was going to execute a plan that was so stealthy, Melissa wouldn't know what hit her. My plan was simple—just be nice. Melissa was crazy... literally.

What better way to drive her crazier than to be nice to her—especially in front of her family—and then do just enough on the down low to make her think she's losing her mind. A misplaced set of keys here. Shadowy figures there. Just enough to make her natural craziness spill like beer from a frosty mug. Before long, she'll start questioning her own sanity and offer Suni to me.

Applying the Sun Tzu's quotes to Gerald was equally simple. All I had to do was make sure he wasn't aware of my plans to drive Melissa over the edge.

In theory, your spouse should be your greatest confidant. However, I'd lived long enough and watched enough reality television to know that some secrets are better kept buried. I had a plan to wrestle complete custody from Melissa for once and for all, but I had no plans to tell Gerald about my intentions. Why? Because of our personalities. He was in Martin Luther King, "turn the other cheek" mode. Me, on the other hand, had the spirit of Malcolm X coursing through my veins. And whether right or wrong, I intended to get full custody of my daughter, "by any means necessary."

Chapter 14

MELISSA

When Ryan first called and said that Suni would be coming to spend the weekends with me on a regular basis, I was skeptical. Well, more than skeptical, I was suspicious. But I wasn't going to let my distrust of him deprive me of seeing my daughter. Maybe the judge's stern words had gotten to him. If that was the case, I could play nice too—all while still wishing him dead.

Judge White was correct with everything she'd said. We had both watered down our part in the fighting. I wanted and tried to provoke Ryan into hitting me, but if the truth were told, he was the one doing the provoking. He knew it didn't take much to make me go left, yet he came over in a fireball acting a damn fool. But in the end, the judge's words that we didn't love Suni more than we hated each other was the razor-sharp truth. I didn't want that to be our story and I had to believe that ultimately, Ryan didn't want that either.

I had no problem focusing on my love for Suni more than my hatred of him, but he made it damn-near impossible whenever he stabbed me in the back—and my back was covered in scars. However, I was willing to do whatever it took to make life good for Suni.

The first weekend, since that ugly day a couple of weeks ago, Suni was coming to spend time with me, I tried to think of some fun things for us to do. The weather would be unseasonably warm, bright with clear skies.

"I think I want to take Suni to play putt-putt golf this weekend," I told my mother over the phone. "I'm trying to think of some fun things to do when she gets here Friday evening." I sat behind my desk with a ton of work in front of me, struggling to concentrate on it.

"I know you do but maybe you two should just stay home—have quality time. Kids don't need as much as we think they do," her soothing voice came through the line, even though I could tell she was a little worried. "Maybe you could do her hair, polish each other's nails—something like that." Mama exhaled.

"But I want her to have a good time while she's here."

"Let him have the Disneyland home and you have the *real* home. Stop trying to compete with Ryan. You're Suni's mother and nothing can top that."

I knew she was right, but I just didn't believe hanging out at home with her would be enough. "Maybe I could take her shopping—to a movie—something."

"Just stay home and relax, sweetie," the worry was becoming more and more clear in Mama's tone. She was trying to prevent one of my episodes.

There was no chance of that, so I conceded to ease her mind. "You're right. I want her to spend as much time at home as possible."

While finishing up my call with Mama, I searched the internet for things we could do inside. It felt silly but I didn't want to blow it. I felt like I had so much making up to do but had no idea how to expedite that process.

I ended my call just as an alert for an email from Ryan came through on my phone. I stood, made my way to the ladies' room as I read it from the small screen.

> Melissa,
>
> If we're still on as planned for this weekend, I'll drop off Suni at 7 pm on Friday, picking her up at 6 pm on Sunday. If anything has changed, please let me know.
>
> Cordially,
>
> Ryan

I knew what he was doing, leaving a paper trail. No problem, I was with that shit too. I promptly replied that all was good, and I'd see them then. Even though I didn't trust him, it was refreshing to have harmonious communication with Ryan, and I felt hopeful that things were working out between us.

On Friday, I took off work early and went to the grocery store, buying all Suni's favorite snacks—string cheese, corn chips, granola bars, and lime sherbet. I even bought cookie dough, thinking she and I could bake cookies together. My last stop was the beauty supply where I picked up all kinds of hair products and nail polishes so we could have a spa day at home. I agreed with my mother on us staying in and spending personal time together. Besides, I wanted Suni to get used to being there again and the best way for that to happen was for us to actually be there just like old times.

Suni never got a chance to get used to her newly decorated bedroom before my breakdown and I wanted to make that up to her. I had already spruced it up so it would be ready for her when she arrived. I even hung new clothes in her closet for her and covered the bed with new stuffed animals.

When I arrived home, feeling better than I had in a long time, I spotted Ryan's BMW sitting in front of the house, to my surprise. It was only six-thirty, so I didn't know what to think when I saw that he was early. However, I wouldn't dare complain. I opened the garage, pulled in, and stepped out my car. I waved for them to come in and started removing the shopping bags from my backseat.

Suni slowly made her way through the yard and up to me.

"Hey, sweetie. How's it going?" I asked her, wrapping my arms around her small shoulders.

"Okay," she barely said.

I pressed my lips to her forehead. "Here, help me bring in these things," I said, handing her a couple of grocery bags. "I have some of your favorites."

I couldn't help but notice her somber mood as she went in through the back door but knew I could turn her frown upside down as soon as that ass of a father of hers left.

"Hey," I said dryly, as Ryan approached holding Suni's suitcase.

Dressed in his Brooks Brothers suit, I assumed he had come from the office. "You are already starting off on the wrong foot," were the first words out of his mouth.

"What are you talking about?" I tried to say as pleasantly as possible.

"Um, I told you we'd be here at six o'clock. We've been sitting out here for over thirty minutes—you could've let me know you were running behind."

"Hold up—you told me seven."

He placed the suitcase on the garage floor. "No—six." He exhaled loudly. "Look, forget it. But if something changes on Sunday, let me know ahead of time. My time is as important to me as yours is to you." With that, he turned on his heels and stormed off.

I was about to just blow it off but remembered specifically that the email he'd sent said seven. I'd verify it later but first I needed to properly greet my girl and tell her all the things I had planned for us.

"Suni-bunny, where are you?" I sang out after stepping through the back door. "Look what I got you—all your favorites."

Slowly, Suni came around the corner.

"There's corn chips and sherbet," I announced. I stacked food from the bags on the countertop but stopped when she spoke again.

"I don't eat that stuff anymore. Daddy G only lets me eat healthy snacks." She took a seat at the counter on one of the barstools.

"Well, you're home now and can eat whatever you want."

"That stuffs not healthy for me."

I paused and thought for a moment. "You don't have to eat any of this if you don't want it." I continued emptying the bags. "What kind of stuff would you like?"

"Veggie chips and maybe some fruit," she said barely above a whisper.

"Okay, we can go back to the store tomorrow. But for now, let's put your things away." I closed the freezer, picked up her suitcase, and nodded at her to follow me. I felt her resistance but didn't know what it was about. It didn't matter, I worked to soften her up.

I could hear her steps behind me. "Is everything okay? You seem quiet."

"I don't know."

I opened her bedroom door and turned to her, catching a glimpse of her face as it relaxed when she took a look around. "What do you think?"

"It smells good in here." She touched the comforter, and then bounced upon the bed.

"It's peaches and coconut." I took in a deep breath. "Air freshener." I pointed to the wall flower in the socket. "What do you think about doing our hair tonight, and then tomorrow we'll do our nails? I bought new hair products I want to try out."

Suni fought back a smile. "I go to the beauty salon now."

"I know you do—and you still can but this weekend we'll have fun doing our own hair. You help me with mine and I'll help you with yours. What do you say?"

The corners of her mouth slowly turned up and I was delighted.

"Should I ask my daddy first?"

"No," I said quickly and then thought it through. I cleared my throat and opened her suitcase. "When you're here, all you need is my permission but if you want to run it by your dad, go ahead. That's fine, sweetie."

With Suni's head covered in hair curlers, and mine in a plastic processing cap, we sat across from each other in my bedroom with two hairdryers humming. She was watching a movie on my iPad and I was on Instagram on my phone. I noticed she was snacking on the corn chips, but I decided not to say a word.

Earlier, I'd watched her devour the tacos we made together, and it was like old times. She ate three of them and considered a fourth until I stopped her. I knew it wouldn't take long to get back to her old self, but I decided to wait to bring up the cookie dough sitting in the fridge.

I closed Instagram and opened my email. I wanted to verify that Ryan *had* told me seven o'clock. I scrolled through three days of emails searching for the one he'd sent but couldn't find it.

Maybe I deleted it and forgot, I thought. I went to the trash folder, but it was nowhere to be found. *Oh yeah, I replied so it has to be in the sent folder, right?* There was nothing there either. *Did I imagine that email?* I thought for sure I had received an email from him and responded to it. Emailing me wasn't his customary way of communicating, but I thought he was trying to do something new—keeping things professional. *Where is that damn email?*

I came out from under the blazing-hot hairdryer with hair treatment escaping the elastic band, dripping into my eyes. I continued scrolling while pacing back and forth, dabbing at my eyes, using the towel around my neck. I went downstairs to the dining room and booted up my laptop, thinking that maybe from a computer screen I'd see something that wasn't coming through on my phone's Gmail app.

Suni was deep into *Toy Story* and hadn't even noticed I'd left the room. I sat at the dining room table, combing through my email. I meticulously viewed my inbox, trash, and sent folders in my Gmail account. I then searched other email accounts, some I hadn't opened in months. *Was it an inbox message on Facebook? Where the hell was that email?*

My plan was to forward Ryan's own email to him, proving that I hadn't been wrong about the time. But then, I started questioning everything. It wasn't a big deal and I didn't want to make it one, but when I couldn't locate it, I went over and over in my head, reading the email and me typing the response. *How could there be no trace of it anywhere? Was it a text he'd sent?* Since I was on my phone, maybe I'd been confused about it being an email.

I thumbed through messages from the last few days and there it was. A text from Ryan with the simple message, 'We'll be there on Friday at 6' was sitting there. It wasn't highlighted so I had obviously opened it and read it. I wore out the floor while pacing, trying to remember. I hadn't responded to the text. I honestly didn't remember getting a text but clearly, I was wrong about the email and the time.

"Hey Mom, my dryer finished." Suni startled me, standing in the entryway of the dining room.

"Okay—let's rinse my hair first and then we'll take down your rollers." I shut down my computer and put my phone on top of it. "Your hair is going to be so cute."

We trotted back upstairs to finish our beauty shop play day. I decided to let the missing email go.

Suni dug into her waffle once she'd covered it with whipped cream. I had never let her eat this poorly before, but I wasn't about to restrict anything she wanted. We slept in—together in her bed—so our breakfast could really qualify as lunch.

I pushed a glass of milk towards Suni so she had something with which to wash her food down. While mine was still in the iron cooking, I grabbed my bottle of Lithobid to take the prescribed capsules with my breakfast only to find it empty. I had just filled the prescription earlier in the week—a thirty-day supply. I double checked the date on the label and saw it was the right bottle.

I kept a reserve in my purse, so I wouldn't miss my dose, but I had to figure out later what had happened to my full bottle. I took a couple of pills out of my purse, swallowed them with some orange juice, and raced back to my overcooked waffle.

I tossed it in the trash and started over, pouring more batter onto the sizzling-hot waffle iron.

"Mommy, your phone is ringing," Suni said with her mouth full.

I could hear it upstairs, so I darted up to my room, making it just in time.

"Hello." I sat on my bed, trying to catch my breath.

"Yes, this is Miranda from Dr. Steiner's office."

"Hi, Miranda."

"How are you today, Melissa?"

"I'm good. How are you?"

"Fine, um... The reason I'm calling is because we've received a message from the pharmacy that you requested more medication. Is there a problem? You should have enough to get you through the month..."

"I hadn't requested a refill—but..." I stood at the foot of my bed.

"You didn't request the refill?"

"No, but I did just notice that I was out... I just got this prescription so..."

"You're out of medication?"

"Maybe I just misplaced it—I don't know." I took a seat on the bed's edge and zeroed in on my socked feet as I thought back.

"Have you been taking it as prescribed?"

"Of course—I mean, yes."

"Hm... Well, let me check with Dr. Steiner on what we should do from here on out. I'll call you back."

"But, just to clarify, I did not call in for a refill. I'm sure I just misplaced the pills that I had... Or something..."

"Mom. Something's burning," Suni yelled from downstairs.

"Oh, shit." I jumped up and started down the stairs.

"I beg your pardon?" Miranda required.

"I'm sorry, I forgot I was cooking."

"Okay, I'll be back in touch with you once I've spoken to the doctor."

I tossed my phone in the pocket on my pajamas. The smoke detector sounded off all over the house as the kitchen filled with smoke. I unplugged the waffle iron and opened a window. The alarm continued to wail so I went to the garage to get the ladder. The twelve-foot ceilings I loved, proved to be a problem for a situation such as this.

Suni held her hands over her ears. Seeing her suffer made the situation more urgent. I climbed up the ladder and first tried fanning the smoke away from it. When that didn't work, I tried taking it down with a broomstick handle. Ultimately, the batteries fell out and the cover was hanging from the ceiling.

Silence.

"Are you okay?" I asked her.

She nodded and then rubbed her eyes.

"Let me open the backdoor—get some of the smoke out of here." I turned on the fan over the stovetop before opening the door. "It'll be aired out shortly, okay?"

She nodded again.

While I worked to clear the smoke, my mind went back to the empty pill bottle and the pharmacy saying I'd requested a refill. I was certain I hadn't, but what happened to the full bottle I'd just gotten? I decided I would deal with it on Monday, after my time with Suni was over. I wanted her to have my full focus. I wanted her to want to come back home to live with me and too much drama would work against that.

I loaded the dishwasher, ate a cold Pop-Tart, and Suni and I finished each other's hair. All was back to normal.

It was cool and cloudy on Sunday morning, but we managed to make it to Sunday worship—albeit late. We sat behind Mama in her wide-brimmed hat, matching her royal blue dress, and Daddy in his wool gray pinstriped suit, up front sitting with the other deacons, listening to the tail end of the sermon. I tried concentrating but was a bit nervous about Ryan coming to pick Suni up later, praying silently that it wouldn't be a repeat of the last time. I truly didn't want any drama. Quietly, I asked God to help me through the transition. Ryan was critical and nasty towards me. It seemed that anything I did wrong was magnified, with him waiting to pounce right on it.

After the benediction, we hung around long enough to greet a few fellow churchgoers, and then hugged Mama and Daddy, saying goodbye.

"You know I cooked enough dinner for you two to join us," Mama said, disappointed that I'd turned down her offer for meatloaf and potatoes. It was tempting but I was tired of using them as a crutch.

"Next time, Mama. I promise. I'm cooking a little dinner myself and then Ryan will be coming."

"Do you need me to be there? It's no problem," Daddy whispered in my ear.

"Thanks, Daddy. We'll be fine."

"You call me..."

"I will, I promise."

He kissed my cheek and then kissed Suni's.

I could see the worry in his eyes. "Everything's been going fine. Don't worry."

Daddy simply nodded and escorted us out the door and watched us make our way to my car.

When we arrived home, I placed pork chops I'd prepared earlier into the oven. I put potatoes on the stove to cook and then mash, and then I put some fresh green beans in the sink to rinse.

"Do we need to look over your homework again?" I called out to Suni who had run straight upstairs to her room. I loved having her home even if it was only for a short while.

When she came down with her backpack, I felt warm inside. She was a good student—it was in her genes—but I did appreciate Ryan making sure she received the best education. It was one of the few things he and I agreed on where she was concerned.

She sat at the kitchen table, working her math problems, keeping me company while I cooked our dinner. Every so often, I stepped over to her to answer a question or just to make sure she was finishing her assignment correctly.

"Dinner is ready," I announced just as I pulled the grilled pork chops out of the oven.

I turned the mashed potatoes on low and placed a spoonful of the sautéed green beans onto two plates. I turned off the oven, forked up a chop, placing one on her plate and two on mine. I then put a heap of potatoes, drizzled with butter, in the center.

"Clear off your papers and let's eat."

Suni closed her books and stuffed her backpack with everything on the table.

"Can you pour our drinks and grab some silverware?"

Suni got right to it. "Mommy, next time I'm here, can I have a friend over to spend the night?" She set the table with a fork on one side of our plates and a knife on the other. She then took her seat and picked up her fork, starting in on her mashed potatoes.

"Hold on, let's say grace," I said and bowed my head. "Dear Lord, thank You for this food we are about to receive for the nourishment of our bodies. Amen."

"Amen," she echoed.

"A friend like who?" I sat across from her and cut into the tender meat.

"Jarelle."

I knew Jarelle and her parents, but I was apprehensive about being responsible for other people's children while I was still in the process of getting better.

"Maybe she can come over for a visit, but I don't know about sleeping over."

"Why not?" she asked quietly.

I understood her needing to be around other kids and that she probably didn't get too many opportunities at Ryan's. I would definitely make that happen next time, but no one overnight.

"How about this... Maybe next time we can go skating or to a movie and you can invite her."

The corners of her lips turned up into a smile.

I exhaled and continued eating. It was almost time for Ryan, but I didn't want to rush Suni but still needed her to be ready when he arrived. I couldn't have him lingering longer than necessary.

Once we were done eating, I cleared the table and sent her upstairs to finish packing up her things. I wanted her bags to be waiting by the front door.

I went back to his text message and realized there was no pickup time, only a drop off time. In that vanished email, I thought it said he'd be here at six but then everything had become questionable.

I dashed up the stairs and double-checked her suitcase.

"If you take any of the things that I bought you, you have to leave something behind, okay?" I had explained earlier that I wanted to be certain that there were always clothes for her—at her real home.

It was six o'clock sharp when the doorbell rang. We went down the stairs, carrying her things, only to discover that the main level was once again clouded in smoke.

What the hell?

"Go let your father in," I said as I raced to the kitchen.

The next thing I knew, there was fire coming from under the pot of mashed potatoes and Ryan rushed passed me and threw a towel over the dancing flames.

"Did you forget you were cooking something?" he asked.

"No, I cooked earlier but I turned off the stove." I noticed the burner was turned to high heat. "I don't know how that happened."

"Are you both okay?" Ryan faked a couple of coughs. "Open the door or something."

I was already about to do just that.

"What's going on with your smoke alarm?" He pointed to the ceiling where it dangled from a single wire.

"Oh, it went off yesterday and I couldn't get it to stop so I disarmed it."

"So, you guys slept here last night with no working smoke alarm?"

I could hear the accusation in his tone and felt a fight brewing.

"Well, just the one night." I pointed to the ceiling just as he had. "I'll have to get someone to come out and reset it for me." I folded my arms across my chest and finished up with, "It was just one night."

"One night is all it takes, Melissa." He then grunted like a raging bull.

I wanted to cuss his ass out but thought about the prayer I had offered up to the Lord during church service.

"And now the kitchen is about to burn down. How could you not know you still had the stove on?"

"It was an honest mistake that could happen to anyone." I hated explaining myself to him. But whatever it took to keep the peace, I was willing to do. "You know, you're right. I need to be more careful." I glanced over at wide-eyed Suni. "Sweetie, are you okay?"

Suni nodded and zipped up her coat.

"Everything is fine, and I'll see you in a couple of weeks." I followed them to the front door, kissed my girl's cheeks, and hugged her as tightly as I thought she could stand. "I love you."

"I love you too, Mommy."

They trotted across the lawn and got in Ryan's car as I watched. I closed the door and silently thanked God that my strong urge to kill him was subdued. There was a lot to be thankful for.

I had been on the phone all morning—or should I say on hold all morning. I was on my third cup of coffee and glad to be getting ignored by most of my coworkers. My work had piled up again, but my new dilemma facing me was paramount.

On the way to work, I stopped to gas up. I thought my bank card was damaged when the system kept denying my purchase. It was just gas. Eventually, I scraped together some bills and paid cash. When I called the bank to order a new card, the bomb was dropped on me.

Even though I had yet to figure out the prescription fiasco, which I was in a hurry to get to my desk and call the pharmacy, I had to put it on hold when I discovered my checking was $1337 in the hole. And that didn't include the insufficient funds fees that were racking up. The killer was that the bank said I had logged in online a week ago and moved $2800 from my checking account into one of my savings accounts. An account I had forgotten I even had.

I argued with them as long as I could until the back and forth became ridiculous. I had spoken to several supervisors, and other people in charge, but we were getting nowhere. This was yet another incident of me wondering if I had done something I hadn't remembered. My stomach turned with me feeling sick with worry. *Did I do this? Did I empty my bank account? Did I throw out my pills and try to order more? Am I experiencing time lapses?* What about that email I swore I'd received from Ryan? *What is really happening in my life?*

"Ma'am, are you sure you're the only one with access to your accounts?"

"Yes, for the fiftieth time," I said, holding the phone away from my ear, yelling into the end of it.

"When was the last time you changed your passwords?"

Something clicked, but before I could linger on that thought...

"Melissa," Jake, my boss, said as he stood behind me. "Can I speak to you in my office?"

"Yes, sure," I responded aloud but, in my head, I said, ...*the fuck now?*

Chapter 15

RYAN

"We need to talk. And I wanna talk right now, Ryan, so stop what you're doing."

"Gerald, I can't sit on this phone with you. I've got a lot going on over here. I've got a hearing to prepare for and little time to do it. On top of that, I've got to go into this meeting with Lofton and sit there while he embarrasses the attorneys who have been underperforming. And I happen to be one of those attorneys this month."

"That ain't my problem, Ryan. We still need to talk."

I let out a loud sigh hoping that would make Gerald back off, but he reminded me of who I was dealing with.

"I don't give a damn about you sighing. You can fall asleep holding the phone for all I care. What I do know is that you're gonna hear what I have to say."

"Look, I don't know what this is about, but I can tell from your tone that you're mad. Whatever it is, I didn't do it."

"So, I guess what I'm lookin' at right now is not your handwriting."

"I don't know what you're talking about. Be more specific."

"Okay, I will. I'm sitting here in your office reading your notes on a sheet of paper. You know... the notes where you planned out how you're going to win Melissa's kindness and then do sneaky shit to make her think she's crazy."

"You're going through my stuff?"

"No, I was cleaning up this junky-ass office. It looks—and smells—like a pigsty. I wanted to get some housework done before I go to run some errands and pick up Suni from school. While I was grabbing the candy wrappers off your desk, I noticed these notes you scribbled on this yellow note pad."

"I don't go through your shit. Why are you going through mine? Just own it... you were snooping."

"Okay, I'll own it... I was snooping. There, I said it. Now that I've owned it, I need you to stop trying to deflect, Ryan. Why are you going to this extreme?"

"All is fair in love and war."

"Excuse me."

"You heard me. I love Suni and this thing between her mother and me is war." I could feel a headache coming on. I opened my desk drawer and downed three Tylenols—with no water. "Look, I intend to do whatever I need to do to get custody of my daughter."

"That's the dumbest shit I've ever heard you say, Ryan."

"That's your opinion. I've gotta do what I gotta do."

"Even if it means compromising your integrity. The man I fell in love with would never do anything this sneaky. The man I fell in love with focused on doing the right thing... at all times."

"Gerald, when we met, I wasn't fighting for my child."

"You still aren't fighting for your child."

"What do you call it?"

"You're acting like a man who has forgotten what's most important. You're more concerned about being right, instead of doing right. And I don't like this side of you."

Before I could reply, Gerald hung up the phone.

I don't need this shit, I thought and hung up.

To say I was distracted was an understatement. My case load was piling up. My billable hours were lower than ever. And the senior partner who lobbied the hardest for me to join the firm, Gabe Lofton, gave me the evil eye every time he walked past my glass-walled office. My performance was less than stellar. But embarrassing yourself is one thing; embarrassing the boss who went to bat for you, is another.

With a pencil in my right hand and my finger-tips burning a hole in the deposition that I held in my left hand, I tried my best to concentrate on the task at hand. When the phone on my desk rang, I jumped.

"Ryan, there is a Mr. Guy Carter here to see you," said Martha, the receptionist.

My heart rate quickened. My hands became so sweaty they left damp prints on the desktop. Never in a million years did I expect a visit from Melissa's father. He'd gone out of his way to let Melissa and me deal with our problems. Showing up at my office was an indication that his approach had changed.

"Umm, tell him I'm in a meeting or something."

Martha's voice lowered to a whisper. "He says it's urgent. He's kind of fidgety. Should I call security?"

"No, he's harmless. I just need a few minutes to clean off my desk and get myself together. Tell him to have a seat and I'll be out in a few minutes."

When I hung up the phone, I started cleaning my office like a young soldier who'd been told the Drill Sergeant was coming. Before things went south between Melissa and me, her father was more of a father to me than my own. I had the utmost respect for him. The tiff between his daughter and me put a strain on our relationship, but that would never stop me from being respectful toward him.

With my desk looking half-way presentable, I used the reflection from my office window to examine my attire. I popped a peppermint in my mouth and devoured it while I made my way to the lobby.

You got this, I thought. *If he attacks me, there are enough people in this building to keep him from killing me.*

"Surely, you're not leaving right now?" said a voice from behind.

"Oh, no, Mr. Lofton. I have someone waiting to see me in the lobby."

"Good. I noticed your billable hours have taken a dip for two months in a row." He sipped the cup of coffee he held. "I expect more from you."

"Yes, they have, sir. But I just picked up two new clients this week. So, you should see a spike soon."

"That's good to hear," the stumpy man with the cowlick said. As he started to turn the corner he said, "You know I vouched for you."

You never let me forget it, I thought.

I'd lied about picking up two new clients; which meant my next few weeks would be spent attending every business mixer and symposium I could find. I intended to pass out enough business cards to wallpaper an auditorium.

When I made it to the lobby, I immediately made eye contact with Martha. Like a bank teller trying to clandestinely finger a bank robber, she nodded in the direction of my surprise guest.

"Mr. Guy," I said as I approached, "is everything okay? Did something happen to Ms. Liz? Melissa?"

He held up his hand and stood up. Even though he was in his early sixties, the man was as lean as many thirty-year-olds I knew. A handsome man who was always dressed to a tee, Mr. Guy had a presence about him. He could very well have been mistaken for one of the firm's senior partners.

"Everything is fine, son. I was just hoping I could steal a moment of your time; just wanna talk to you for a few minutes."

I looked over at Martha, the company gossip. She nearly snapped her neck trying to look away and pretend she wasn't eavesdropping.

"Yeah, sure. C'mon, let's go to my office." I opened the door that led from the lobby to the hallway where our offices were located and waved him in. "Martha, hold my calls, please."

"No problem, Ryan."

I walked ahead of Mr. Guy and led him to my office. As we entered, I saw Mr. Lofton peering around the corner. He had no idea who my visitor was, and I sure wasn't going to tell him. I needed him to believe Mr. Guy was one of the two new clients I'd lied about.

"Wow, this is a nice office. It's bigger than our first apartment." His head swiveled. "Leather sofa. Television. Son, you've made it to the big time."

"Yeah, I can't complain."

"All the walls are glass. You must feel like you're working in a fishbowl."

"Please sit down, Mr. Guy." I walked around my desk and sat down. "Yeah, it does feel like a fishbowl. Unfortunately, it's kind of a reflection of the times we're living in. People are quick to scream sexual harassment these days. I guess the firm figures the glass walls will keep everybody honest—no way to do anything inappropriate in the workplace when anyone walking past can see inside."

Mr. Guy nodded in agreement. He held his trade-mark Kangol style hat in his hand, rubbing his fingers across the bill as he stared at it.

"You want something to drink? I've got water and a few Cokes in this little fridge here."

He waved dismissively.

"Okay," I said and grabbed a bottle of water from the refrigerator for myself. His unwillingness to make eye contact with me was unnerving. After a while, I started to wonder if he really did have a gun or some other kind of weapon inside his jacket. I cleared my throat. "Umm, Mr. Guy, no disrespect, but I got a lot of work to get to. I know you didn't come all the way down here to talk to me about my glass office. What's on your mind? Did Melissa ask you to come here today?"

Mr. Guy smirked and spoke while he looked down at his hat. "No, Melissa doesn't know I'm here, so don't hold that against her. Hell, my wife doesn't even know I'm here. She thinks I'm at the auto parts store buying something for my old truck."

I could feel my nerves starting to rouse so I grabbed that pencil I'd been using before he arrived and fiddled with it to give my hands something to do.

"Do you remember the day you asked my permission to marry Melissa?" He looked up at me. "'Cause I do. It took you thirty minutes to get around to saying what was on your mind that day. Truth be told, we knew what y'all were gon' announce the minute you came in the house."

"Was it that obvious?"

"As obvious as a bump on the tip of your nose."

"Me and Melissa rehearsed all the way over there. I knew my lines until y'all answered the door." I could feel the tension in my face giving way to a smile. "Yes, I remember that day well. I was so scared to see y'all that day that I turned the car around and drove back to my house to change shirts because I had sweat stains in my armpits."

"Yeah, you looked more nervous than a cat in a room full of rocking chairs."

"I was scared you were going to snatch me by the collar and beat the crap out of me. I was ready to make a dash for the front door."

"Hell, it wasn't me you needed to be worried 'bout. Liz has always been the judge and jury in my house. She was the one who wanted to beat you."

"Yeah, Ms. Liz grilled me like she was the lawyer and I was the one on the witness stand."

"She was just being a mother. And mothers are protective of their kids."

I may have been reading too deeply into his remark, but I felt like it was a double entendre.

"I agree, Mr. Guy, but some of us dads are just as protective of our kids—and our roles."

"You ain't gotta convince me, son. You can search high and low and you won't find a bigger advocate for father's rights. Some of these women act like carrying the baby for nine months gives them parenting seniority. They tend to forget that if it wasn't for our contribution, they wouldn't have a baby to carry around for nine months. There isn't a baby on this planet that's ever been born without a man's sperm."

"Amen," I said.

Mr. Guy looked at me and smiled. "Do you know that I've always liked you?"

"Yes, sir. You and Ms. Liz have always made me feel accepted."

"After you and Melissa told us y'all were expecting a child and we sat in that living room and asked y'all a million questions about y'alls future, Liz and I had a long talk when y'all left." Mr. Guy stood up and started to pace. "Here's something you don't know."

"What's that?"

"We suspected you might be gay."

I'm not sure what my facial expression was when he said that, but I'm sure I looked like a man who'd been forced to inhale air in a room full of used jock straps.

Mr. Guy leaned on the glass wall and looked at me. It was like he was eyeballing my soul. I suspected he could tell I was getting nervous because he offered a tension breaking chuckle and said, "Close your mouth, son. You gon' let a fly in."

"I'm... I'm just surprised to hear that. I didn't know. Melissa never told me."

"Because we never told Melissa." There was a twinkle in his eyes. "Nah, there are some things parents should keep from their kids. Especially, when you don't have any concrete proof. You know what I'm saying?"

Damn, a second double entendre and he ain't been here five minutes, I thought.

"I hear you."

"Actually, Liz is the one who brought it to my attention. She said she saw something in your mannerisms. Her biggest concern was whether you were man enough to be a good protector for our daughter and grandchild."

"Did you share that concern?"

"No, I didn't. I told Liz that you got our daughter pregnant, so you were clearly man enough to make a baby. And based on the conversations you and I had about life and your plans, and even your childhood, I felt like you were man enough to take care of my daughter and grandchild."

"Thank you, Mr. Guy."

"Unfortunately, I feel like I was only half right."

I leaned back in my chair. "Excuse me."

He started pacing and then stopped and said, "I was right about you being a good protector for my grandbaby. Yeah, there is no doubt in my mind that you'll walk through fire wearing gasoline drawers for my precious Suni." He moved toward me and stopped next to the side of my desk. "But I was wrong about your ability to take care of *my* baby, Melissa."

"No disrespect, Mr. Guy, but Melissa isn't my responsibility anymore."

Mr. Guy shook his head pitifully and looked at my degrees hanging on the wall behind me. "All this education and you don't get it."

"Don't get what?"

"Son, you may not be married to my daughter anymore, but she's the mother of your child. That means, to some degree, she's still your responsibility."

"But I—"

"But nothin,' son. If the mother of your child ain't doing well—emotionally, financially, spiritually, or mentally—that means your child ain't gon' do well. You know why?" he asked rhetorically. "Because kids aren't stupid. And my beautiful Suni, damn sure ain't stupid. When she's with you, she's gon' be thinking about her mother. Your primary job as a father is to provide for your child's emotional and financial needs. Now, there ain't no arguing the fact that you got the financial part down pat." He waved his arm while he turned slowly to admire my office. "I mean, look at ya'... big time attorney with your fancy office." He pointed at me with his hat holding hand. "But a *real* man takes the most pride in conducting himself in a way that would make his child proud. You're supposed to be the standard for your daughter, the benchmark that your daughter compares every man she meets."

As if Mr. Guy's tongue lashing wasn't enough, Satan decided to serve me a second helping of stress. My boss walked past my office, tapped the glass, and pointed at his wristwatch.

"I see the *man* is breathing down your neck," Mr. Guy said.

"Yeah, I have a meeting to go to in a few minutes. He's a stickler for everyone being on time. If you're five minutes early, you're still ten minutes late to him."

"Sounds like the boss I had before I retired. The worst micromanager ever."

"Yeah, he's a pain in the ass, but what can I do... he's the boss."

"The clowns may change, but the circus remains the same. My advice...get all the knowledge you can out of these folks and then get the hell out of here and start your own firm. As long as you're punchin' another man's time clock, you ain't never gon' be free from the bullshit." Mr. Guy put his Kangol on and strolled toward the door. As he grabbed the doorknob, he looked at me. "Can I give you one more piece of advice before I go?"

"I've always listened to your advice," I said and stood up. "No need to stop listening now."

"I can't, and I would never, tell you to stop fighting for custody of Suni; that child is just as much yours as she is Melissa's. All I ask is that you fight like a man... and not like a bitch."

I sat mannequin like for a few minutes after Mr. Guy left my office. My hands were pressed against the top of my desk. My eyes were glued to the door. And my body was tethered to my leather chair because it's hard to move when someone you respect has just verbally rammed his foot up your ass. Unfortunately, Mr. Guy's lecture was a day late and a dollar short. I'd already started fighting and put some things in motion that my smooth-talking, ex-father-in-law would have surely classified as *bitch-like*.

Chapter 16

MELISSA

Three framed pictures of Suni, two coffee mugs, a crystal guardian angel figurine, and other whatnots from my desk were in a box in the trunk of my car, which was parked in my garage. I couldn't bring myself to carry the box into the house. How will I explain losing my job? How will I hold onto this house I'd fought Ryan for and won? How can I legitimately fight for custody of Suni if I can't even provide for her financially? No judge was going to be okay with that.

I was just starting to get back to myself, or so I thought, when I got fired. I still hadn't gotten the prescription thing sorted out and was out of medicine, and I could feel reality slipping away. I desperately wanted to hold on to my sanity but that was rarely a fight I won.

I had been lying in the bed for a week, keeping phone conversations with my parents short and keeping to myself in general. My doctor didn't believe that I'd misplaced every pill bottle I had and wanted me to come in for an appointment. I knew what that meant. If I showed any signs of instability, he'd be trying to send me off somewhere. So, the last time I spoke to him, I told him that the pills had been found and I was back to regularly scheduled doses. All lies. But I couldn't risk being hospitalized again. Those events were just too hard to bounce back from so I would will myself to stay sane until it was time for a refill.

Unfortunately, every day that I avoided people, the more ill I felt. I was losing objects daily—keys, the remote control, a glass of juice or water, lapses in time, missing money from my bank account only to have it reappear—it was crazy, or I was. I even felt like someone was watching me, and being paranoid was not something I'd struggled with in the past. I tried my best to ignore it and willed myself to hold it together.

It was three o'clock in the afternoon when I gathered every ounce of strength in my body to lift my head from my pillow. My legs felt like cement blocks when I pushed them over the side of the bed. I was tempted to crawl back under the covers, but I forged ahead and stood to my feet, putting one foot in front of the other, making my way to the bathtub.

While the water ran, I took fresh, non-matching bra and panties out the top drawer in the closet and pulled my favorite Black Panther t-shirt off a hanger and tossed all of them, and a pair of jeans, onto the counter next to the sink. The whole time I moved about, I peered over my shoulders, expecting to see something but not sure what. I closed the bathroom door securely—stopping short of locking it—slipped out of my night gown and stepped into the hot water laced with bath oils.

The weight of my situation was becoming clear. I had wasted a whole week sulking about the loss of my job. I hadn't started looking for something else and I hadn't even filed for unemployment. Surely, I had that coming to me and I needed to get that money rolling in because bills and car notes wouldn't wait. I inhaled the scent of teakwood and musk, leaned my head back, closed my eyes, and made a vow to get started first thing Monday morning, working on my resume and getting my life back together.

After soaking and relaxing in the water until it turned cool, I lathered up, rinsed off, and stepped out. I dried my body and covered myself in lotion. Standing naked in front of the mirror, I could see that the pounds were slipping away. The medication made me hungry, so I guess losing my appetite was inevitable. I wasn't mad about that.

I reached for my clothes only to find a matching set of underwear and a yellow sundress next to the sink. *What the hell? Where are my jeans? Where is my black t-shirt?* I gathered up the things and went back to the closet and found my Black Panther tee hanging on its hanger. Slowly, I placed my hand on it while clearly remembering pulling it off the hanger. *Did I hang it back up and choose something else?* It wasn't even warm enough to wear a sundress so why would I...

I hung the dress back on a hanger and stepped into the jeans and t-shirt that I thought I'd originally picked out. Feeling like I was in the Twilight Zone, I combed my hair, put on a little make up, and prepared to leave the house. It was my weekend with Suni, and I told Ryan I'd pick her up. I wanted to be on time, with minimal drama.

I trotted down the stairs and went to the sofa table where I normally left my purse and keys. They weren't there. I searched the room, and then checked the dining room. I could hear a low hum coming from the kitchen. When I passed the stove, I could feel heat rising from the oven. On the island, my Cuisinart Mixer was running and next to it, an opened box of cake mix I was saving for Suni's visit. The carton of eggs sat open and an empty measuring cup was there too. *What is going on?*

I checked all the doors and they were locked just as I'd left them. The garage door was down and absolutely nothing else seemed amiss—except it appeared I'd started trying to bake a cake. Tears welled up in my eyes. *Am I seriously losing it? Do I need supervision? Should I check myself into a hospital?*

I emptied the batter from the mixing bowl into the sink, threw the box and discarded eggshells into the trash can, turned off the oven, and wiped down the counter. I spotted my purse and keys sitting at the kitchen desk and just as I was about to pick them up and head out, the doorbell rang.

Quietly I crept to the foyer. I could see Sherry Agnew, a former co-worker and longtime friend, through the peephole. *What does she want?* I hesitated. I didn't feel like answering a thousand questions. She'd left the Kroger company a year ago and had most likely gotten the word I'd been let go. She had been there for me during my divorce, but we'd drifted apart once I had been hospitalized.

While I stood at the door thinking, I could hear her footsteps going down the porch. I exhaled and waited to hear a car drive off. But then, there was a knock at the back door. Why wouldn't she just go away? *Okay, let me get this over with.*

I made my way to the back door, wearing my jacket and with my purse on my shoulder and keys in my hand. I snatched open the door and before I could say a word, she spoke up.

"Girl! Here you are."

"Um, yeah... Hey Sherry, what's up?"

Sherry rocked back and forth, balancing her 150 pounds on feet that seemed too small for her body's 5'11" frame.

"How's it going? How's Bill and the kids?" I tried making small talk.

Keys jingled in her hand as she pressed them against her chest, and she appeared to be out of breath.

"You okay?" I asked.

Sherry made her way by me and stepped into the kitchen.

"The question is, are you okay? I've been calling you for months now and I know you got my messages." Her sandy-colored dreadlocks that were short the last time I saw her were now hanging past her shoulders. Dark freckles peppered her pale skin and she smelled of coconut oil.

"Oh, sorry about that. It's just been crazy around here." I still had my hand on the doorknob of the opened back door. "Hey, I'd love to chat, but I was just heading out."

"Don't play with me, Melissa. How are you doing?" Her arms folded across her flat chest as if she were in a standoff with me. "Are you and Ryan okay? What's going on—y'all back together or something?"

"The hell. What made you ask some shit like that?" I closed the door.

"Well, I just saw him leave from here. For a minute, especially when you didn't answer the door, I thought I was gon' be on a future episode of *Dateline*. I know that motherfucka' is crazy. But now I see you answering the door all *shower fresh*, I thought maybe his gay ass was tryn' to revert back." Sherry's infectious laugh filled the room and I noticed a bit of nervousness in her chuckle as she relaxed.

I wanted to join in her laughter but what she said had me perplexed. "Wait, wait, wait just a damn minute. Ryan was here just now?"

"Yeah, I saw his sneaky ass rushing up the street to where he parked his car. He got in his BMW, made U-turn, and turned the corner." Sherry stretched her arm, pointing in the direction he'd left. "Girl, when you didn't answer the door at first, I thought, aw fuck. I'm gon' have to call 911..."

I stood peering through Sherry while she continued, as thoughts filled my head. There was absolutely no good reason for him to be at my home and I knew Sherry wouldn't mistake him for somebody else.

"You okay, sis?" she asked me.

"Hey, I got to get out of here." I noticed the clock on the stove read 6:30. "Is that right?"

Sherry held up her wristwatch. "Naw, it's only 5:30. Why?"

I then looked at the time on my cell phone and she was right. Why was the stove's clock an hour off? Yeah, some shit was finally making sense.

"Girl, I'm sorry but I have to get going." I opened the door to the garage and hit the button for it to open. "I promise I'll do better at staying in touch."

Sherry followed me into the garage. "Okay, you know I worry about you. Don't hesitate to call if you need me." She opened her loving and wiry arms and stepped in to embrace me.

I hugged her back and it felt good. I promised myself, in that moment, I'd call her more often and fill her in on everything that had been going on. She'd been a dear friend to me, and I hadn't shown my appreciation by being there for her.

"I love you, girl," she said as she made her way down the driveway.

"Love you, too—maybe we can get the kids together this weekend," I yelled out and opened my car door.

Sherry waved her hand and got into her Honda. I sat behind the wheel listening to her tires crunch loose gravel in the street. I inhaled and exhaled slowly but it didn't seem to help. I went over every detail of the things that had been happening to me and most of it had Ryan's name on it. My head was swirling while thinking of how devious and diabolical a person he was. I started the car and threw it in reverse.

The discrepancies at the bank. The missing emails. The missing medication. The missing keys. The missing time...

I turned a few corners, picking up speed, all while my blood was boiling. I didn't know how he'd pulled off all of the antics, but I could guess on a few. It was my mistake for not changing passwords, PIN numbers, and the locks on the doors and simply giving him the benefit of a doubt. He had moved on with his new lifestyle and you would think that would be enough for him. No—he wanted to drive me crazy and take my daughter away from me. How could he be so heartless?

I parked my car at the curb in front of Ryan and Gerald's townhome and marched across their perfectly manicured lawn. The next thing I knew I was banging on the door, calling for Ryan to bring his punk ass outside. I didn't have to wait long before he swung open one side of the French doors and my fist landed dead in his mouth before he could utter a word.

"I know it was you; you sneaky son of a bitch." Then I grabbed his necktie and pulled him all the way out of the house.

Ryan tried grabbing my arms to contain me, but they were flailing out of control. "You crazy bitch.

What's wrong with you?" He turned and yelled toward the house, "Gerald, get your phone and video this fool." He was trying so hard not to hit me back.

I didn't let up; one more hook to the side of his face. "I know everything—everything you did to me."

"You're paranoid—Gerald," he yelled just as he grabbed my arm, body slammed me face-first and straddled my torso, holding me down.

While I was eating grass, I caught a glimpse of Gerald and Suni rushing out of the front door.

"What the hell are you doing, Ryan?" He had his phone in his hand but slipped it into his pants pocket.

"Get her on video—get her on video."

Gerald turned and pushed Suni back into the house. "Stay inside, sweetie." He marched to the front yard and pulled Ryan off me with ease. "What are you doing?"

"She sucker-punched me and I'm tired of her putting her hands—"

"You and your man can both go to hell. I know what you've been doing," I yelled while getting on my feet and spitting dirt out my mouth.

"You're crazy."

"You want me to *think* I'm crazy. Sneaking into my house—"

"Give me the phone, Gerald. I want to get this on tape."

"What's she talking about?" Gerald asked Ryan.

"Oh, don't act like you didn't know he's been trying to make me think I'm losing my mind—taking money from my bank account—throwing out my pills..."

"She don't know what she's talking about. She *is* out of her mind," Ryan insisted while trying to move past his husband.

Gerald stepped between us and turned toward me. "Money from your bank account... What's going on here?"

"For weeks now, this bastard had me thinking I was crazy—misplacing things, keys, my phone—all kinds of shit. But he just left my house—somebody saw him with his car parked down the street." I swung on Ryan again, but Gerald caught me by the wrist. "I knew you could do some low-down dirty shit but even this is low for you." I tasted blood so I touched my swollen lip. *Had he hit me?*

"Lies, all lies. Tell her I was here all afternoon, tell her."

I snatched away from Gerald and punched Ryan dead in the chest.

"Give me the phone, I'm calling the police," he said to Gerald.

Gerald stepped back, securing the phone in his pocket, and that's when I noticed him looking toward the house. My eyes followed his and I saw Suni standing on the porch, crying her eyes out.

"Look what y'all doing to Suni. Come here, sweetheart." Gerald rushed to her, picking her up and turned back toward us. "When are y'all gonna learn there's something bigger at stake than your petty differences. I'm not calling the police, and," he continued, staring Ryan in the face, "I'm not lying for anybody."

"Daddy—Mama, please stop fighting," Suni managed to get out between wails.

I stepped toward Gerald and reached out for my daughter.

Gerald pulled back and said, "I'll take care of Suni. Y'all handle that." He nodded toward the street.

A police car was at the curb and two officers were getting out, watching us closely.

"Do the right thing," Gerald said to Ryan and headed inside, carrying a crying Suni.

All I could think was, *I'm headed back to jail.* The fuck.

"Sir, is everything all right here? We got a call from your neighbors." The two male officers approached but only one spoke up. "Ma'am?" The brother stayed back with his hand resting on his weapon.

"Everything's fine," Ryan started out nervously. "I'm attorney Ryan Gray with the Troy Law Firm. My ex-wife and I were having a loud disagreement; you know how it is."

"Ma'am, are you okay?" the same officer was doing all the questioning.

I nodded and waited on Ryan to throw my ass under the bus, telling them how I'd come over there to jump him, get handcuffed, and promptly thrown in the back of the squad car. *Damn.* I knew he would, it was his specialty.

"We were having an argument, but everything is fine now," Ryan answered for me.

"Let's let her answer," the officer said. "Ma'am?"

"I'm fine," I began, "I'm just here to pick up my daughter—it's my weekend visit." Blood dripped from my lip onto my hand as I pointed toward the house.

"Are you injured?" the officer asked me. "Is that blood?"

The policemen promptly separated us, taking our individual accounts of what had happened. The words of the judge resounded in my head about how she didn't want to hear any more about us fighting. We promised her we wouldn't—both of us. I stuck to the story that neither of us had hit the other, assuming Ryan would go along. But being the punk that he is, he told the cop I'd come over there and attacked him. One thing led to another—he looked fine and I had a busted lip, they believed that I was covering for him and thought he was trying to blame everything on me and next thing I knew, Ryan was in handcuffs and being hauled away. I wanted to do a happy dance but, I held my composure.

"What happened?" Gerald burst through their front door, racing towards me.

"He's headed to jail, that's what. I know you don't believe me, but Ryan has stooped to the lowest this time—all to keep my daughter from me."

"I don't know why you two can't just get it together and put her first. Why is that so hard? I know neither of you mean to hurt her but all the fighting—it affects her well-being."

"Look, I'm here to pick up Suni. Can you please go get her?"

Gerald exhaled as loudly as he could, turned from me, and went inside the house. When he returned, I hugged Suni, put her in the backseat, and closed the door. I faced Gerald and said, "Look, I hear you and I don't doubt that you're right. I have enough problems in my life without Ryan adding to them, trying to make things harder for me. I don't want to fight him but sometimes he leaves me no choice." I placed my hand on my door handle. "I'm sorry for today and for what it's worth, thank you for looking out for her." A single tear escaped my eye and I could see compassion on Gerald's face. "I really do appreciate it."

I slid behind the wheel, looked at my broken-hearted daughter through the rearview mirror, and started my car. It wouldn't take long for Ryan to O.R. out of jail, and I prayed he wouldn't come knocking on my door soon after. I truly did want the fighting to end.

Chapter 17

RYAN

The group, TLC, had a popular R&B song in the 90s called, *I Ain't too Proud to Beg*. If there was a contest to find a song title to best describe my behavior in the back of that police car, that TLC song would have won by a landslide. The judge made her intentions clear when we left the courtroom the last time. We could both lose custody of Suni. So yeah, I begged—no, that's not a strong enough adjective—I pleaded for those cops to not take me to jail.

The black officer drove the car. While I implored them to cut me a break, I couldn't see his beady eyes behind the lenses of the shades he wore, but I could see his head twitch—from the road ahead to the rearview mirror and back to the road. He was mean mugging me the way a man in a physical altercation with a woman should be mean mugged. The other officer, a white man, is the one I decided to focus on. I couldn't tell his age, but the streaks of gray in his hair and the stripes on his shoulder suggested he was the older and more seasoned of the two. My mind went into overdrive.

This black cop seems like he just left the academy. The first thing he did when he got out the car at my house was place his hand on his weapon. This white boy was relaxed from the moment they arrived, like he'd seen this all before.

The brotha has no stripes; the white cop does. The brotha looks like a damn MMA fighter; the white cop looks like the only thing he curls are beer cans after work. The black cop is wearing a shiny wedding band— it's got that "just got married" glow; the white cop has no wedding band—not even a ring tan or print on his ring finger.

If I'm going to avoid being locked up, I'm going to have to appeal to this white boy because this brotha looks like he wants to "Rodney King" my ass.

"Officers, I don't know if y'all have ever had baby-mama drama," I said while focusing solely on the white cop, "but if you have, you know how the male is always painted to be the villain."

"So, she made her own lip bleed?" asked the black cop sarcastically.

"Not deliberately, but the answer is *yes*. She was swinging wild and I was blocking the blows. She may have hit herself. I know I never threw a blow—you can interview every neighbor out there and they'll confirm that." I shifted my focus to the black cop. "Officer, I'm an attorney. I know when I have the upper hand. Why would I do something to ruin my leverage? She came to *my* house raising hell."

"Why?" asked the white cop.

"She's mad that I have been granted primary custody of our daughter." I knew that I needed to get more info about my audience, so I dangled a little verbal bait for them to nibble on. "Y'all may not know the significance of that, but trust me, that's not a privilege that's granted to most men."

"Trust me, I know," the white cop muttered.

Bingo. I've found his sympathetic sweet spot, I thought.

"You been through a custody battle before?" I asked.

"Yep," the white cop replied. "Been there, done that."

"The system is bias as hell," I said. "You can catch a woman with a damn crack pipe in her mouth and the courts are going to find a way to give her the benefit of the doubt. The fact that the judge granted me custody should let y'all know how mentally screwed up my ex-wife is."

The white cop glanced over at the black cop. He didn't say anything, but his eyes said, *He ain't lying.*

Got'em, I thought and went in for the kill.

"Hell, she predicted this shit would happen."

"What?" asked the white cop.

"When she was bangin' on my door and demanding to see our daughter—even though it's not her week—she told me that if I didn't step outside to talk to her, she'd raise hell and claim I beat her."

"That's not what she said," the black cop chimed in. His tone dripped with animus. He'd been silent the entire ride. His comment caught me off guard. "Matter of fact, she kept tellin' me nothing happened between the two of you."

Shit, Ryan... think fast.

"Officer, she was once the wife of an attorney. She's never been to law school, but she's heard enough of my cases to know how the game is played. My ex knows she doesn't have to *say* I did anything. It's human nature for people—especially policemen— to side with a woman who looks injured in cases when there is a domestic dispute. I get it... cops have wives, daughters, and sisters. Your instinct is to protect the woman. The problem is, there are a lot of manipulative women out there who know that they'll get the benefit of the doubt when the cops show up."

Neither commented. I need to drive my point home with a mightier blow.

"Look at who y'all are taking to jail—the man. Not the woman who was the aggressor; the man who did nothing more than try to protect his face from the blows she threw." I offered a disconsolate chuckle for affect. "Yeah, she wins again. Called her shot like Babe Ruth in the '32 World Series. Got me arrested and now she has possession of the child that the judge awarded to me. I swear... a brotha can't win for losing."

Other than the sound of the dispatcher's voice barking out incidents and locations for "calls for assistance," the car was deafly silent. One block. Two blocks. Three blocks. The car moved like a barge trudging down the dirty Mississippi river. I started to feel like my plea had fallen on deaf ears when I heard the white cop say, "Pull over in that parking lot."

The black officer pulled into the parking lot of a Tom Thumb grocery store. The two officers got out the car and talked in the parking lot. They were out there long enough for the white cop to pull out a cigarette and take a few drags.

I wasn't sure what to expect when they got back in, but I hoped and prayed something I said would tether us. After all, they may have been police officers— trained and conditioned by society to be emotionally disconnected, especially when dealing with black men—but they were men long before they put on those uniforms. My experience as an attorney taught me that I didn't have to convince them I was right, I just needed to create enough of a *reasonable doubt* in their minds as it pertained to Melissa. If they could find even a hairline fracture in her story, it might be enough to evoke some level of empathy within them.

"All right," the white cop said. "My partner and I have talked about it. I'm going to give you a break today. He thinks it's a bad idea," he said pointing at the black cop without looking at him, "but I'm the senior officer here, so I'm making this call. If I have to come back to your house for another domestic violence call, I'm telling you right now... not only are you going to jail, but the ass-whooping you're going to get during the ride is going to be one you'll never forget."

"I understand. I promise you won't have to come back to—"

"Shut the fuck up," the black cop barked.

The officer turned the car around and started on the ten-mile trek back to my house. When we turned on my street, the block looked desolate. I'm sure one of my nosey neighbors noticed me being dropped off by the police, but that embarrassment I could handle; it beat having to look that angry judge in her eyes and try to explain why Melissa and I were fighting again.

I thanked the officers—neither acknowledged me—and got inside my house as fast as I could. The heat from their lazer-like gazes on my back made me wince. I didn't feel like the bullseye was off me until I closed the front door.

The air conditioner wasn't on, but there was an arctic chill. The smell of herbs and spices would normally grab my attention, but the air was stale.

"Gerald?"

My voice echoed. There was no reply.

I could see our bedroom light on and saw flashes of Gerald's shadow against the wall.

"Hey," I said.

Gerald spun on his heels with his hand pressed against his chest. "You scared the shit out of me. I thought they took you to jail."

"They let me go," I said flatly. My eyes were affixed to the chaos before me. There were clothes all over the bed. "Good thing they didn't take me to jail because it doesn't look like you were coming to get me. What's up with all this?"

"What does it look like?" Gerald placed a suitcase on the bed and opened it. While stuffing clothes inside he said, "I'm leaving you."

"Why?"

"Because I'm tired of this shit."

"I didn't do anything. She came over here."

"She came over here because you were snooping around her house like some type of creep." He stopped packing long enough to look at me. "You carried out that dumb ass plan you scribbled on that notepad, didn't you?"

"Look, I'm not proud of what I did, but I felt I had to."

Gerald shook his head and stared at me in a way I'd never seen. It's the kind of disappointment that always precedes a breakup. Anger is a secondary emotion, it's always the byproduct of some type of core act that causes embarrassment or feelings of disrespect. Anger is fleeting; therefore, when couples break up amid anger, they often get back together once the core issue is addressed. When your partner isn't angry, but disappointed—rarely is there any coming back from that. Disappointment goes bone marrow deep. You lose something worse than blood—you lose respect for those who disappoint you.

"The fact that you felt you had to is what gets me. Ryan, you're not the man I fell in love with. Honestly, I have no idea where that man went. I guess I need to come to the realization that he's nothing more than your representative. This is the real you."

"I know, I have—"

Gerald held up his hand. Brick wall.

"Ryan, I really don't want to hear it." He looked at me. "I don't care anymore."

Gerald walked to the closet and grabbed an arm full of clothes that were on hangers. He tossed the hangers on the bed each time he removed an item, folded the item, and shoved it in the suitcase. When he tried to close it, it looked like a child who'd stuffed a hamburger in his mouth.

"Let me help you."

"Don't touch me... or any of my shit... again."

Gerald didn't raise his voice, but he was emphatic. The room felt colder.

"Ryan, I promised I'd be by your side during this fight, but I never promised to sit back and watch you fight dirty. I'm not saying Melissa is a more fit parent, but I will say this, you ain't much better than her. And if I should be asked to testify in court during that custody hearing, that's exactly what I'm going to say. Neither one of you deserve to be Suni's parent right now."

The suitcase landed on the floor with a thud. He lifted the retractable handle, scanned the bedroom, and then looked at me. "I'm leaving you... for good. I'll always love you, but honestly, I no longer like you. And I can't be with someone whom I don't like."

I reached for his hand, but he swatted it away. I could feel a breeze as he moved past. It was the kind of breeze that doesn't just close a door, it slams the door. Our relationship was over.

"Suni wrote a paper in class last week," Gerald said from behind me. I don't believe he turned around—his voice sounded distant. We stood back to back—him leaving and me staring at what would now be a bed that I'd sleep in alone. "In two hundred words or less, she had to say what she'd do with a million dollars. She got an A on the paper, but she was afraid to tell you or her mother about it."

"Why?"

"Because her wish involved you and Melissa."

"Did you read the paper?"

"Yes. She let me read it yesterday."

"What does it say?"

Gerald's sigh sounded like a snake's hiss.

"Ryan, you asking me that question cuts to the core of why I'm walking out this door. You let pettiness distract you from being the type of father that child needs. If you wanna know what's in the letter, man up, start acting like a *real* dad, and read it your damn self. It's on her dresser."

I sat on the bed in shock. Water-filled eyes darted around a bedroom that would no longer be privy to Gerald and me discussing plans, our favorite television shows, politics, and things we like and don't like about the people we know and don't know. Luther Vandross was right when he talked about a room not equaling a house and a house not being a home. Those were lyrics that I heard, sang, and grooved to, but didn't *feel* until the love of my life walked out my life and didn't look back.

Still reeling from having my heart mangled, I staggered over to Suni's bedroom. Her scent—a pleasant mixture of dandelions and cotton candy—lingered. Lavender from wall-to-wall. Matching pillows and a white bed spread with a huge unicorn on it—its silhouette traced in lavender. Suni's vision brought to life by Gerald's flare for design.

The paper that Gerald spoke of sat on the dresser. It seemed to be calling out for me like the smart kid in class who nearly throws an arm out of socket trying to get the teacher to call on her.

Yeah, I see you, I thought.

After wasting a few minutes peering and touching items in the room that were irrelevant at that moment, I picked up the attention-seeking paper. The first thing I noticed was the huge red "A" in the top right corner. Next to the grade was a smiley face in the same red print and a message: *Great job! Be sure to show this to your parents!*

I used the heels of my hand to dab my eyes. Suni's combination cursive and print writing style appeared three dimensional. It was as if her spirit was in the room saying, 'Nigga you gon' read this letter whether you want to or not.'

Suni's canopy bed squealed from my weight. Its cry was drowned out by the loud thump of my racing heart. My mouth was dry as cotton, and my normally steady hands trembled violently. The moment I dreaded had arrived.

If I had a million dollars, I would buy something to make Mommy and Daddy happy so they can stop fighting all the time.

I would buy Mommy a house and a car to make her happy. I would also help her get a boyfriend because I think she hates my daddy since their divorce. I would send her on a trip to Paris. She always talks about going there someday.

My daddy is a lawyer. I don't think he needs a lot of stuff. He is always laughing and smiling when he is around my Uncle Gerald. When he is around Mommy, he changes. He's mean and he yells. He curses a lot too. It scares me when he gets like that. I think he needs a vacation. I heard him talking about how beautiful the pyramids are in Egypt. I think that's where I would send him with a million dollars. It would make him happy and when he came home from vacation, he would be nicer to Mommy.

I'm not sure if money can make people be nicer to each other, but that is what I would do with a million dollars.

I've never been kicked by a mule, but I doubt if the blow hurts more than Suni's words. To know that the child, whom I loved more than I loved myself, believed I was a mean man who hated her mother and needed a vacation so I could be happy, shook me to my core.

Psalms 8:2, states: *Out of the mouth of babes and sucklings hast thou ordained strength.* I can admit that prior to reading Suni's paper, that scripture, for me, was like the speech flight attendants gave before takeoff—you hear it, but you don't. Suni's letter was a cry for help. Her teacher's note next to the grade was a passive-aggressive call for Melissa and me to pull our heads out of our asses and recognize the pain we were causing our daughter.

Suddenly, I was motivated to do that which anger had prevented me from doing—bury the hatchet with Melissa.

I showered to wash away the madness of the day and headed out the door. Melissa often went to her parents' house in times of distress, so I decided to head over there first. My hunch was right. Her parents' car was parked in the driveway, crooked, as if they were in a hurry to get inside.

I could hear faint sounds behind the door when I knocked. I figured they were debating whether to open or call the police. Just as I was about to turn and walk away, the door opened, and Mr. Guy stood there with an intensity I hadn't seen before. He was prepared to protect his daughter—by any means necessary.

"Why are you here?"

"Mr. Guy, I didn't come to fight. I didn't even come to get Suni. All I want to do is give this to Melissa."

"What is it? Another threatening letter from your attorney?"

"No, sir. It's written by Suni." I gave him the school paper. "It's an assignment she wrote in class. I just read it. And... And for the first time, I... I can honestly say, I want this fighting to stop."

Mr. Guy read the paper. I stood before him like a child waiting to be punished by the school's disciplinarian. Frown lines appeared and his eyes closed as if he was struggling to keep all that he wanted to do or say inside.

"Wait here," he said and closed the door.

I stood outside for what seemed like ten minutes before the door opened again. When it did, I was surprised to see Melissa standing there crying. At first, I thought she was going to come outside, but she gestured for me to come in.

Ms. Liz stared at me from her spot on the sofa. Snarling. Her eyes flickered with angry flames. I couldn't tell whether she'd read the letter, but if she had, her granddaughter's words only made the stern matriarch's animus toward me grow. I sat in a high-back, claw foot, chair positioned just out of her reach. If she lunged at me, I'd have time to get out the way.

Mr. Guy, whose face seemed somewhat softened, sat on the arm of the sofa with his arms crossed—the queen's sentinel.

"It hurts me to read this," Melissa mumbled.

"It hurts me too," I said. "Look, Melissa, at this point, I'm tired. I became obsessed with winning custody. I had it in my mind that I was the better parent—the one who could provide the most stable home for Suni. What I failed to realize—and what her letter showed me—is that her seeing two parents who love and respect each other is more important than us being in competition."

"I agree," Melissa said.

"I just want us to get along." I realized as I was saying it that I sounded like Rodney King during his infamous appeal for peace during the Los Angeles riots. "Suni's happiness is all that matters to me now. Even if it means that she lives with you full-time, I want what's best for her," I looked directly at Melissa and continued, "and for you."

Melissa sobbed openly. I could feel her pain. Each tear that dropped on her cheek singed my skin. For the first time in years, I hugged my ex-wife. I could feel her body go limp in my arms. The emotions swept over the room because from my periphery I noticed Ms. Liz dabbing her eyes with a piece of tissue. Mr. Guy slid from the arm of the sofa and draped his arm around his wife. I struggled to hold back my own tears, but my effort was futile. They flowed like the Nile River. Down my cheeks, along the ridge of my chin, and settled on the top of Melissa's head, which rested on my chest.

Suddenly, the wave of pain that swirled around that tiny living room parted like the Red Sea. It was God—in the form of Suni.

"Daddy," she called out.

With Melissa cradled in my arms, I reached for my daughter. Suni ran over and wrapped her tiny arms around her mother and me.

"Please, stop fighting," she said, her words drowning in her tears.

I released my hold of Melissa and knelt. I held Melissa's hand and Suni's and said, "I promise you, baby. Your mother and I won't fight again. We read your school report and we *heard* you."

Epilogue
MELISSA

With a microphone in his hand, looking open-casket sharp in a tuxedo, Ryan stood in front of a roomful of my father's friends and loved ones, singing Daddy's praises. It was Daddy's 65th birthday celebration. There wasn't a dry eye in the room.

We were all dressed to kill in the ballroom of the Adolphus hotel in downtown Dallas. Mama and Daddy sat at the head table with Suni right next to them. The room was slightly lit, and the band was taking five while a spotlight was on Ryan.

"Most of you know I lost my parents..." Ryan's voice cracked, and then he cleared his throat and continued, "never getting to meet their only grandchild, they were snatched from this earth. But when I found myself all alone, Melissa's parents stepped right up and took me in as their son, and I will forever be grateful for that. Even when Melissa and I didn't make it, Mr. Guy never showed me anything but love—even when things got ugly. I know everyone has their own experience with this great man but speaking on behalf of everyone in the room and for those who wanted to be here and couldn't," Ryan turned to Daddy and continued, "happy birthday and may God bless you with health, happiness, and many more years to come."

The room erupted in applause and I watched my father dab at the tears escaping his eyes. My mother leaned over and pressed her lips against his just before Daddy grabbed Suni, placing her on his lap.

Suni was the only kid in the room. We wouldn't dream of celebrating Daddy without her there. Dressed in lavender chiffon, she lit up the dance floor most of the night, hanging on to her grandpa. She was the star of the night and the magic in all our lives. The one thing we all agreed was paramount in the family— Suni's wellbeing.

Talk about being broken down... I never imagined I could feel so ashamed, but when I read Suni's school report the words made the reality of my actions clear. It didn't matter when Judge White told me I had placed my disdain for Ryan over the love for my daughter. No, that didn't impact me. When my father pleaded with me to scale back the fighting, I ignored him too. Even when I saw my life falling apart before my eyes, I forged ahead, trying to ruin Ryan.

Hearing Suni's pain in the words she wrote was like a red-hot, serrated knife being plunged into my chest. What had we been doing to our precious baby? I couldn't believe that we had both—not just Ryan— sank so low in how we behaved in front of her.

When I thought back on the day Suni was born, I remembered the plans and goals Ryan and I had set for her and ourselves as parents. We would do whatever we could to give her the best education, make her feel secure as a female of color growing up in a country that offered plenty of opportunities and would give her unconditional love and care. Those were only some of the promises we made on that day and we had abandoned all of them as they became lost in our acrimony.

Now there are new promises, healing, forgiveness, and rediscovered priorities. Our family therapist is seeing that we keep them. We even wrote a contract with specific guidelines to adhere to and it has been the sanest thing Ryan and I have ever done—certainly over getting married in the first place. Life is good again. My medication is managed, I have a new position with an old employer, Suni is her old self, and Ryan even seems content even though he and Gerald never reconciled.

"Hey, Daddy." I placed a loving arm around my father's shoulder just as the band returned to the stage. "It's almost ten o'clock, and time for me to take Suni home."

"Aw, can't I stay a little longer?" Suni looked up at me with her sleepy, big brown eyes, pleading.

"Girl, you'll be asleep before we turn the corner. Kiss Nana and Grandpa and go tell your dad good-night."

I watched a pouting Suni do everything I asked her to do and realized my heart was full. There's laughter and a warmness that we haven't shared in years. Mama and Daddy have their son again and I have my friend again. Life with us is better than it's ever been—healed in only the way an innocent child can heal.

About the Authors

BRIAN W. SMITH, in 2004, endured a personal trauma that inspired him to write his first novel, *Mama's Lies–Daddy's Pain*. In 2005, he formed his publishing company, Hollygrove Publishing, and in 2006, self-published the semi-autobiographical novel. The novel sold thousands of copies. Brian capitalized on that success by transitioning from a self-published author to an Independent Publisher of more than 20 novels for himself and other authors.

In 2008, Brian scored his first Dallas Morning News Best Sellers with his novel, *Nina's Got a Secret*. The novel was also listed in Oprah Winfrey's, O Magazine, on the "What to Read" list. Since then, he has written other critically acclaimed novels that have earned spots on the Dallas Morning News, Amazon, Target, and Black Expressions best sellers lists. In 2011, he sold the rights to *Nina's Got a Secret,* to Strebor/Simon and Schuster. Brian has been named Male Author of the Year by multiple review organizations and has been a Featured Author at numerous Literary Events (e.g., National Book Club Conference, National Black Book Festival, etc.). His novels have appeared on numerous best sellers lists to include: Amazon, Dallas Morning News, Target, and Black Expressions.

When Brian is not writing novels, he serves as an Adjunct Professor of Creative Writing. Brian is a native of New Orleans, La., and currently resides in the Dallas, Texas area.

www.AuthorBrianWSmith.com

ELAINE FLOWERS is not only a professional writer of mainstream fiction, she is also a professional book editor and publisher, residing in Addison, Texas. She became a published author in 2004 and in 2006 was Interim President of The Writer's Block, Inc., an organization of black writers in the Dallas metroplex. This is where Elaine gained her experience critiquing other author's work, later launching her own critique group that was active for five years.

During that time, with the release of her *Dallas Morning News* bestselling novel, *Black Beauty* and went on to pen nine more books. Flowers' latest book, *Bigamist* continues to receive 5-star reviews. In 2019 she was awarded Author of the Year from Black Pearls Keeping It Real Book Club. She is also Chief Operating Officer of a book publishing company, where she helps other writers realize their dream of becoming published.

Elaine holds a Bachelor of Fine Arts degree in Creative Writing for Entertainment from Full Sail University and resides in Texas.

www.booksbyElaineFlowers.com